Millie —

SMOKY MOUNTAIN STORIES

Back to Tennessee. Enjoy!

ALSO BY JERRY PETERSON

Novels
Early's Fall
Early's Winter
The Watch
Rage
Iced
Rubbed Out
The Last Good Man
Capitol Crime

Short story anthologies
The Santa Train
A James Early Christmas
A James Early Christmas II
The Cody & Me Chronicles
Flint Hills Stories
Fireside Stories
A Year of Wonder

Stories I Like to Tell
– Book 2 –

SMOKY MOUNTAIN STORIES

JERRY PETERSON

WINDSTAR PRESS

Copyright 2017 c̲ Jerry Peterson
Windstar Press

All Rights Reserved.

ISBN-13: 978-1977584533
ISBN-10: 1977584535

Cover Design c̲ Dawn Charles at
bookgraphics.wordpress.com

October 2017

Printed in the U.S.A.

DEDICATION

To Marge, my wife and first reader.

To the members of my two writers groups, *Tuesdays with Story* and *Stateline Night Writers.* They are sharp-eyed readers and writers who demand the very best of me in my storytelling and craft of writing.

To a friend and one-time colleague who prefers to remain unnamed.

SMOKY MOUNTAIN STORIES

Movies, Lies & Lottery Tickets

*Note: Some people play the Powerball for something to do. For a buck, it's cheap entertainment. For others—and maybe for you as well—it's serious business.

"DANTE, YOU OUGHTA get ta hell outta here."

Jim Daws—Dante to those who worked at the S&W Grill—glanced back as he shoved a stack of fresh-washed plates wiped dry onto a shelf. "Someday, Mac."

Sorrel MacDonald pulled hard on a pipe wrench—Sorrel, the S of the S&W, a big man in a Titans cap pushed onto the back of his head. "You paid your time in purgatory, my friend, three years. Time for you to go."

Dante, slim, in his mid-twenties, picked up a porcelain soup bowl. A hairline crack caught his eye. No one else would have noticed, but he examined the crack. The dishes he washed and dried, like this one, had a shine on them before they went out in the diner, so customers could see their reflections if they cared to look. "Mac?"

MacDonald felt around the drain fitting under the new machine. "Yeah?"

"Got a crack in this one."

"In what one?"

Dante held the bowl down for MacDonald to see.

He peered at it. "Yup, throw it away. You know the health department rules."

But the kid held onto the bowl, as if it were an old friend. "Maybe we could use it for something else, put flowers in it or something."

"Or those damn Powerball tickets you keep talking us into buying."

"Not a bad idea." Dante rummaged in the back of a silverware drawer where he kept the stash, two hundred eighty Powerball tickets. Granted, they were dead except for the five for this week that he had rubberbanded together so he could find them when the state posted the winning numbers, but the dead ones, he never threw them away. If he put them all in the bowl on end—seeds for their garden of dreams he said every week as he collected a buck each from the other four employees, then added his own. Dante worked the number combinations they would buy—birth dates, first two numbers off someone's driver's license, last two numbers off one of the five one-dollar bills, the phase of the moon plus onetwothreefourfive, somewhere there had to be a system. Somebody always won. Maybe not on the first week, but always.

Eventually.

That was the state's rule.

You could put it in the bank.

The dead tickets did look something like sprouts

when Dante set the bowl up on the shelf over the flour bin.

He looked back to where MacDonald was scrabbling out from beneath the steel counter that hid the plumbing needed to make the new dishwashing machine work. "Mac, you think that thing's going to do the dishes as good as I can?"

"No, but they'll come out sterilized and hot-air dried. Health department has been stripping our hides because we've let you hand-wash and towel-dry 'em. The idea of a few germs scares 'em." MacDonald rubbed the back of his neck. He rotated his head, vertebrae snapping like so much popcorn popping. "Damn, I get stiff when I'm under there."

"Then don't work under there."

"And get a plumber in to do this stuff? Not for what he'd charge."

"Then trade him meals."

"Always with the ideas, aren'tcha?" MacDonald wiped his hands on a shop rag. "Kid, why don'tcha move on, do something worthwhile with your life. I can get a rummy to feed this machine."

"Like the rummies you used to get to wash the dishes?"

"Okay, so nobody's ever been better than you. But why the hell aren't you in college?"

"I'll tell you someday, after we win the Powerball, and we all retire to Virginia Beach."

MacDonald laughed a deep baritone laugh that vibrated everything that was loose in the kitchen. He rumpled Dante's hair as a loving uncle might a favorite nephew's. "At least get the hell outta here for the night.

I wanna go home."

Dante gazed at the stainless-steel box that housed the engineered monster intent on making him unemployed. "Aren't you going to test her?"

"Naw, that kin wait 'til morning when we've got us a stack of breakfast dishes to wash."

THREE YEARS. Dante hadn't kept track of the time, but apparently MacDonald had. Three years, he thought as he shuffled up the stairs to the apartment above the S&W. MacDonald let him have it for cleaning it up and painting. It wasn't much, just a couple rooms, one a kitchen that had a hotplate instead of a stove. The refrigerator was one of those little boxes like college students get—like he had at one time—got it at the Secondhand Rose down the street. But it was enough, the dishes and silverware, and pans and mixing bowls, they were extras from downstairs.

The furniture he scrounged, most of it castoffs people had put out on the curb. The futon, though, that he had bought new with his own money, along with the sheets and blankets and his one pillow. The idea of sleeping on someone else's bed, on someone else's sheets, made his skin crawl.

Supper this evening was a Tex-Mex chili Dante had allowed to simmer all day so the flavors would be at their richest and the peppers at their hottest. He had tried to talk MacDonald into putting it on the menu, had cooked up a pot's worth in the S&W's kitchen, had him sample it. After MacDonald regained his breath and some semblance of a voice, he swore. Tears leaked from his eyes for the longest time.

What Dante couldn't eat, he put in a Tupperware bowl and put that in the box refrigerator. When he had washed and put away his dishes and had wiped down his card table-slash-kitchen table, the light on the Avalon's marque flipped on across the street. The Avalon, a rococo movie house long before even MacDonald was a thought in his parents' minds, became disheveled and dowdy after the mall had been built on the edge of town and a three-plex, the three-plex replaced some years later by a six-plex and, last year, by a ten-plex. To survive, the man who owned the Avalon went to showing second-run movies, then third, now anything he could get cheap enough so the movie house could survive on buck admissions.

That Dante could afford. An inexpensive pleasure. An escape. And since the S&W wasn't open for supper, he had his evenings free . . . and how many times could he read the quartos of Shakespeare's plays that he had found at somebody's yard sale? Downstairs, they had gone to calling him Will because he recited soliloquies from *Hamlet* and *Love's Labour's Lost*. To that he said no, call me Dante. "Really, I much prefer *The Inferno*," he said.

Most of that epic poem he could recite from memory as well.

Dante wandered to the front window and looked out. "Oh my God."

There in letters a foot and a half tall read this night's movie offering, *Before Sunrise*.

Dante grabbed up his jacket and clattered down the stairs. He ran across the street devoid of cars and shoved his dollar bill through the opening in the box-office window. The Avalon had quit issuing tickets long ago. Whoever was in the box office just nodded as he or she put the buck in the cash box and thumbed toward the door.

He went on in, bought a bag of reheated popcorn and a box of jujubes—big spender that he was—and went through the curtain and down to his favorite seat, third row center.

The memories came back in a flood as the music swelled under the opening scene, a train somewhere in Austria . . . Ethan Hawke and Julie Delpy meet. They go to the buffet car, have some coffee and talk. "Why don't we get off at Vienna, spend the night together before I have to catch a plane home to America?" Hawke says.

And they do. They wander the city's streets talking about the kinds of things real people talk about—so sweet, so gentle. There is an attraction, yes, and a first kiss on the same Ferris wheel used decades before in another movie, *The Third Man.*

Dante had caught the train out of Charlottesville after he first saw the movie, to see if he might duplicate it, to see if he, too, might meet someone.

And he did. Lorraine was her name.

And she asked him to come with her to Atlanta, just for a day, maybe two.

And he did, in full knowledge that he was cutting classes at law school.

You missed a test, one of his professors said when he returned. I was sick, Dante said, too embarrassed to say he had gone to Atlanta with a young woman on a lark and love. But he told his roommate, and the word got around, and two weeks later the dean called him in, told him that he had lied to his professors in clear violation of the school's canon of ethics. And the dean dismissed him, stripped him of his scholarship, and banned him from the campus.

All that and yet Dante still loved the movie.

And the girl.

What had become of her?

What had become of him?

He couldn't go home and face his father, a lawyer and judge, a distinguished alumnus of the University of Virginia, the college that Thomas Jefferson had started. So he ran, and he lost himself. Dante couldn't remember in what.

Meth?

Angel dust?

One morning he found himself slumbering in the back doorway of the S&W, only he didn't know what it was or in what city he was, nor did he know the towering giant who opened the door.

Dante found himself MacDonald's project. MacDonald had asked almost no questions and that was a comfort. Months to clean up and shape up, and now why would he ever want to leave for, as Dante viewed it, he had everything one could want—an apartment, a movie palace, a place to work, though his job was about to change and he would now be feeding dirty dishes into a machine.

How long had the lights been up?

When had they come up?

He had only become aware when the ticketseller/

projectionist/janitor nudged him with a broom handle.

"Dante?"

"Hmm?"

"You gotta go home now. I gotta clean up."

Dante forced himself out of his seat and worked his way out to the aisle.

"You didn't spill no popcorn or stick no gum under the seat, didja?"

"No. I never do."

"Like the movie?"

A smile lifted Dante's face. "I did, Sweeney."

"Well, you tell your friends then, all four of 'em, they oughta come."

MORNING CAME early. Must have because Dante woke to the clatter of pans in the kitchen below and someone pounding on the ceiling with a mop handle.

"Get it down here, Dante! We got dishes."

Oh damn.

It was MacDonald.

Dante rubbed at the sand in his eyes and squinted at the Timex clock on the floor beside his futon. Seven-ten. *Hadn't I set the alarm?*

He pulled on his jeans and a tee-shirt, stuffed his sockless feet into his sneakers, and pulled foot for the door and the stairs beyond. When he slip-slid into the kitchen, Arnie, his apron tied up under his arms and his ever-present Tennessee Vols cap backwards on his head, was sweating over the grill, cracking open eggs for someone's order. "Git to the dishwasher, boy. We're gettin' backed up here."

Gladys, the more buxom of MacDonald's two waitresses, bustled in with a tray of dirty dishes above her shoulder. She slung the tray down next to four others stacked with remnants of the early breakfast trade. "Sweetie, how soon can we get some clean ones? We're getting desperate."

Dante tipped the first plate up over the garbage disposal. With his other hand, he brought down a shower head and sprayed off half an uneaten pancake and a chunk of jellied biscuit. "Five minutes if this thing works like the manual says it should." He put the plate in the washer rack and took up another.

"Well, all right, but if we have to break out the styrofoams, you know how mad Mac's gonna be." Gladys tickled Dante's ear, then dashed when Arnie bellowed about an order being up.

Rinse and stack, rinse and stack. The first rack loaded, Dante pushed it through the rubber flaps and into the steel cabinet. "Here goes nothing," he said and slammed his hand on the red START button.

Nothing.

Nothing happened.

Dante punched the button again.

Still nothing.

Arnie elbowed him aside. "Jeez, kid, it's a machine. You have ta show it who's boss." He picked up an empty tray and whanged its flat side against the dishwasher.

The machine spit.

It spit again, scalding water.

The spits became a hiss and the hiss a high-pressure shower, steam billowing out.

Arnie jutted out his chin—the victor—and went back to his grill.

Dante mopped his arm across his forehead. "Damn," he said, "don't let me ever get crosswise with you."

Arnie swiped a slice of Texas bread through an egg mix and dropped the bread on his grill. "Ya learn these things, kid. Ya learn these things."

Dante returned to his rinsing, this time cups and glasses. The manual said the machine was automatic, that there was nothing to do now but wait—and load more racks—while the genie inside spray washed and spray rinsed and spray sterilized, then dried the load with its jet of hot breath and expelled the rack of clean dishes on the other side.

MacDonald peered through the pass-through. "How's it going, kid?"

"You wouldn't believe it if I told you."

"Maybe on break. Holler if anything goes wrong."

Arnie shoved a plate with a short stack, eggs over, and hash with gravy in front of MacDonald. "Order for Holly."

MacDonald took the plate and twisted away. "Holly!"

And so it went. Seven-forty, eight, eight-thirty, nine.

At nine twenty-three, Dante stacked the last of the machine-clean dishes, ready for the noontime rush. He went to the sink and splashed his face with cold water. From there he ambled into the dining area while he toweled his face dry.

"You know," he said to MacDonald, Arnie, Gladys

and Holly seated at a Formica table, each sucking up coffee and chewing on a sweet roll, "that kitchen was hot with Arnie's grill. With the new dishwashing machine, it's a steam bath."

MacDonald slapped an empty chair. "We can get an exhaust fan in there, pull some of that heat out. How about you sit, and Holly'll getcha an iced tea?"

Dante eased his way onto the chair, taking care not to lean back out of fear he might stick forever to the seat back.

MacDonald winked at his project turned good. "Arnie and Gladys want to know if you checked the numbers last night."

Dante slapped his forehead. "I forgot. I went to a movie."

Arnie hunched over his plate and his half-eaten roll, his normal frown turning to a scowl. "Well?"

"I'll get the tickets, okay?" Dante shoved his chair back and ran, ran into Holly on his way to the kitchen. He relieved her of the ice tea. "I love you," he mouthed and went on through the door—back into the furnace—to the flour bin. There he took down his stash. He poked through the passel of dead tickets, searching for the five he had rubberbanded. "They're not here. They're not here!"

"Dante?"

"They're not here!" Sweat beads punched out on Dante's forehead. He dashed back into the dining area, bowl in hand, flicking dead tickets to one side and the other as he ran. "The Powerball tickets are gone! Somebody took them. Arnie?"

The short-order cook threw up his hands, a 'who

me?' expression on his face.

"Gladys?"

"Forget it. I'm like Mac. The odds of winning, we're just shippin' our money to the tax guys in Nashville."

"Then why do you keep giving me a dollar to buy a ticket?"

Gladys sucked on a Virginia Slim. She blew the smoke out from the side of her mouth. "Because you're cute. You remind me of my grandkid."

Dante turned on the one who had gotten him the iced tea—Holly, not much older than he, and every customer's favorite from the size of her tips.

"No. No way," she said. "I'd have to tell Father Mike at confession."

"Then who took them?"

MacDonald made a show of opening the morning newspaper to the page on which were printed the winning Powerball numbers. He patted the numbers and took from his shirt pocket a pack of tickets bound together with a rubberband. "When you kept them in the drawer, I didn't worry. But when you put them out where any delivery man or health inspector might help himself, well—So check 'em, huh?"

Dante ripped the rubberband off. He set the stack of five beneath the winning numbers and read across, one index finger moving under the newspaper's numbers, his other under the first ticket's numbers. "Got a match on one number." But he shook his head and stuffed the ticket into the soup bowl.

Again the index fingers moved beneath the two sets of numbers, a ticket at a time. "No match . . . No match . . . Two numbers here . . ."

Four tickets gone.

Four tickets dead.

Dante wiped at the corner of his eye, stretching his face skin. He pushed the fourth ticket aside, and again his index fingers traced their lines with the fifth ticket. "We got a number . . . a second . . . a third—" His gaze flicked up and down, between the newspaper and the ticket. "—a fourth . . . We got 'em all!"

Dante pounded on the ticket and the newspaper. He twisted them to Arnie. "Check 'em. Check 'em!"

The short-order cook hooked the bows of his glasses over his ears. And he read, his lips moving. "Sonuvabitch. We're millionaires. Mac, I quit."

Gladys pulled the paper and ticket away. She turned them so she could read them, Holly crowding in. "He's right. Fifty-one million bucks. Mac, I quit, too. I'm going to Florida where my kids are."

Holly primped at her hair. "And I'm going to beauty school."

Dante put his hand over the ticket. "Can I ask you all a big, really big favor?"

MacDonald scratched at his mustache. "Depends. Whatcha got in mind?"

"Three years ago, I got kicked out of law school. Now the reason's not important. When we get the check, can I borrow it for a couple days?"

Arnie's frown returned.

Gladys studied the surface of the coffee in her cup.

Holly looked away.

But not MacDonald. He gazed at Dante. "Why?"

"I want to take Amtrak to Charlottesville. I want to wave that check in the face of the dean who threw me out."

McDonald chuckled. "A way of saying up yours?"

"I guess."

"You think Arnie's gonna trust you alone with that check for a couple days? We all go or nobody goes."

Gladys grabbed Dante's arm. "I just want my share as soon as we can get that check to a bank."

MacDonald lifted Gladys' hand away. "Dante, maybe you oughtta think of something else."

HE DRIFTED across the street to the Avalon, to the box office, grubbing out his dollar bill. He pushed it through the opening in the window, but it was not Sweeney who took it.

Dante peered in at a much older man, white haired, the man's face puffy and tired. "Mister Rensaleer?"

The man smiled. "Sweeney wanted the night off, and, since I'm gonna be selling my theater, I thought, what the heck, a night with my customers would be a good thing."

Dante tilted his head to the side. "Really? You're selling?"

He nodded. "I've been here nigh onto a half century, the last twenty-nine years as the owner. Yeah, I love this old movie house, but my kids tell me the time's come to retire."

"You? Retire?"

"I'm thinkin' seriously about it." He came forward on his elbows, close to the glass. "Dante, you're the most loyal of my regulars. Maybe you oughtta buy this place."

"Well, I have come into some money—"

"You're puttin' me on."

"No." Dante gazed around the front entrance, at the movie posters on sandwich boards. "I've seen these old theaters restored, and they become quite something. Have you set a price?"

"No, but I'm open to negotiating. Right now you better get inside. I'm about to start the movie."

The old man slipped away through the box office's backdoor to the stairway that led to the projection booth. As he went up, Dante meandered inside, the theater lights still fully on. He made his way down the aisle, but there was someone sitting in his regular seat—a woman by the cut of her hair.

Dante slipped into the seat beside her. "I usually sit there, where you are," he said as he settled in.

She turned to him.

And he to her. "Lorraine?"

"Do I know you?"

"Jim. Jim Daws." He touched his hand to his chest, his fingers spread wide. "Atlanta. What're you doing here?"

"If you must know, a business trip. I went to Movies Dot Com on my iPad after I got in and saw *Before Sunrise* was playing here. I love this movie."

Luther Click & the Lawman

*Note: Luther Click is one of the first characters I created for what is growing into a series of Wings Over the Mountains novels, Luther, a gentle mountain farmer and a moonshiner. Since just about everyone in any area of the Appalachians where I've lived seems to be related to one another, it just seemed natural that Luther would have a cousin who is the sheriff in his county. That's Quill Rose. Quill, though, is not the lawman in the title of this novella. You'll soon meet that person and Quill, as well.

Chapter 1
Three Crows

LUTHER CLICK abandoned his tow sack when he saw a smoke plume rising beyond the ridge. That smoke—it wasn't natural, not here. Luther knew it.

He tucked the sack and its contents into a laurel bush, then crept to the top of the rise, to an outcropping of rocks.

He sniffed at the air, picked up a curious smell, an acrid smell, and he saw movement some distance below—three men coming out of a thicket. The early morning sun flashed off something on one of the men's jackets.

Luther sank down among the rocks. He hid his presence and waited fully a half an hour until what had been a plume of smoke was little more than a wisp. Luther, glancing around, crept out and made his way down the far side of the slope and into the bush, a rhododendron thicket—the Devil's Taterpatch.

Deep inside, he came on the smoldering ruins of a still—the mash and whiskey spilled, the barrels burned, the copper coil hacked to uselessness.

Luther knew who owned the still and knew the three men who had destroyed it had not caught them. He had recognized one of the three—the sheriff of Blount County, Quill Rose, his second cousin. While the others could be anyone, Luther figured one might be a federal marshal and the other a revenue agent.

"They sure wrecked it, didn't they, Luther?"

He jumped. Luther spun around. "Jesus, J.W., you kin shorten a man's life, sneakin' in like that."

"Easy, friend. You know Daddy was a Cherokee. He taught all us boys to move like we was walkin' on cotton."

J.W. Crowe. His brothers, Leon and Clem, lounged beside him, the trio a nondescript lot except for their hawk noses. Each toted a rifle, its barrel pointed toward the ground.

Luther took their measure. "Were you here?"

J.W. nodded. "We heered 'em coming an' lit out."

"Come on, now. Quill Rose is as quiet as you."

"That may be, but we got us some turkeys in the

patch, and we feed 'em. They really get to squawkin' when strangers come 'round."

"I didn't know that."

"That's 'cause you never come by."

Luther settled back against the trunk of a scrubby tree. "Oh, I've been here a time or two, J.W., but you and your bothers weren't home."

"You didn't leave no sign."

"No sir. I didn't want to attract strangers who had no business to be here."

Leon Crowe pushed the toe of his moccasin at a scrap of the coil. "Like them that burned our still?"

"Like them."

"Wonder how they found out?"

"Leon, like as not, you got somebody mad at you, and they told the sheriff where to find yer place of work."

"Damn. We're sure outta business now."

J.W. Crowe went over to where the mash had been spilled. He picked up a handful and let it dribble through his fingers. "We needed this run of whiskey. We've not had rain for a month at home. Our gardens an' cornfields are burnin' up. We may have nuthin' to go into the winter with. And now to have to buy new copper to make us a coil?"

Luther prodded the ashes of what had been oak barrels. "Well, we can't have yer children goin' hungry. Tell you what, boys, on yon side of the ridge you might find you a sack of whiskey jugs, each one of 'em full. Why don't you take 'em and turn 'em into some cash? That and shootin' some turkeys and deer, you kin get by."

J.W. glanced up. "You make the shine, Luther?"

"Me? That's agin the law, don't you know?" Luther winked at the three Crowes. He turned to leave, but turned back. "I think I'll get me on home. My mules get kinda lonesome if I stay away too long."

J.W. flicked mash into the rhododendron. "Yer a good man, Luther Click."

Luther bobbed his head. He again took a few steps to leave and again turned back. "Boys, you find yerself a new place to rebuild, and you take yer turkey guards with you. You come back here, one morning you're likely to find old Quill waitin' for you. He don't give up easy."

Luther, graying and stooped from his years of farming his rough ground at the edge of Cades Cove, stuffed his hands in his pockets and shambled out of the Taterpatch. He had three ridges to cross and five miles to walk to get home.

The Crowes were a lean bunch. Luther knew why and mused about it as he walked along. Each brother had a flock of children, and they got to the table first.

He didn't have that concern. Other than a team of mules, an old sow pig and her litter, and eight chickens that roosted in the trees in his yard, Luther didn't have anyone, and hadn't for a decade, since Nineteen Sixteen when his father had died at the age of eighty-three—Bernard William Click, a veteran of the Fifth Tennessee Volunteers, a Civil War infantry company that had fought with the Yankees.

Quill Rose, sheriff for only two months at the time of the old man's death, had rounded up a group of veterans from around the county seat and brought them in uniform to the funeral. One, fifteen years younger than Luther's father, had been a bugler in the Fifth Tennessee. He played taps as Luther, his brother Bill, and two farmer neighbors from the cove lowered the box that held the old man's body into the ground.

The old man had given his son two inheritances— his hard scrabble farm and the skill of a mountain whiskey maker. Luther made it a point to be quiet about his business, so only a few knew he had the premier trade in the county. He supplied the judges at the courthouse.

LUTHER HUMMED a Primitive Baptist hymn, *The Lord has been Good to Me*, as he shuffled his way down Gobbler's Knob and around the end of his barn. He slowed more when he saw company standing by the steps to his kitchen porch.

Luther waved to them. "Whatcha doin' here, Quill Rose?"

Rose returned the wave. "Friends and me have been out for a walk. Stopped by to see if we might beg a bite of lunch. Where've you been, cousin?"

Luther came on. "Quill, you know we got kin living on yon side of Big Grill Ridge—"

"The Kirklands?"

"That's them. Just coming home from a visit."

Luther reached out his hand, and Rose took it, gave it a smart shake, the two an odd pair, Luther not much over five feet tall and Rose well over six, Luther in Oshkosh B'gosh bib overalls and Rose in a suit. "How're Earl and Rhella getting on?" Rose asked.

"Just fine. 'Course, they still got that mess of kids at home, and they keep Aunt Rhella pretty well run out, cooking an' washing for them. Who're your friends here?"

Rose motioned them forward. "Seth Watson, he's a marshal. And Avery Bass here, he earns his pay as an alcohol tax agent."

"Yer welcome at my house, gentlemen," Luther said as he shook their hands. "Now for something to eat, tell you what, Quill, why don't you go down to the garden and pick us some greens, and I'll get Mister Watson and Mister Bass here to help me in the kitchen. We'll bake us some cornbread, and I've got a groundhog I killed and skinned last week, baked and set aside, so we'll have us some good country food."

QUILL ROSE came in with a dishpan full of garden and wild greens—lettuce, beet tops, wild mustard, dandelion, and nettle greens—that he had washed at the outside pump. He looked over Watson's shoulder, Watson peeking into the oven. "Smells good."

"Doesn't it, though." The marshal touched the top of the baking cornbread. "It's coming on fine. And that groundhog Mister Click's got in there warming, he says he prepared it with spicewood."

Luther bustled into the kitchen, carrying a tray loaded with jugs and jars he had brought from the spring house. He set the tray on the sideboard and turned back to Quill Rose. "Help yerself," he said, motioning to a black cast-iron frying pan hanging from a nail in the wall, a cup with bacon fat in it beneath the skillet. "Go ahead, them greens won't hop in the pan and cook themselves."

Rose did as he was told while Luther directed the tax man to set the table.

For himself, Luther poured buttermilk from a gallon container into jelly jars.

Rose stood at the side of the stove, stirring the greens. With a fork, he lifted one out and tasted it, smacking his lips. "Uhmm-uhmh, they're ready."

Luther brushed Watson's shoulder as he passed him, carrying the jelly jars to the table. "Cornbread should be ready, too, Mister Watson. Take it out and cut it. I'll get us the meat on the way back."

The marshal found a pot holder. He got the bread pan in it and put the hot pan on the sideboard where he cut the bread as one would a pie.

Luther, towels wrapped around his hands, brought out the pan of meat. As he sliced it, he sampled a piece. "Ummm, Quill Rose, you gotta try this."

Rose helped himself to a bite. He popped it in his mouth and chewed, and a smile spread across his face. "My, Cousin Luther, what you do with spices. I've heard of the term ambrosia. I don't know what it is, but I'm told it's good, and this is good."

Luther ushered Rose to the chair at the head of the table. The others settled to the sides, and Luther, for himself, stood behind the chair at the foot of the table, his hands resting on the back. "You gentlemen ever have sweet pertater butter?"

"Not even heard of it," Bass said.

Luther went back to the sideboard for a crockery jar and carried it back. "Ma taught all us Clicks how to make it. It was kind of a family ritual in the fall when we were puttin' food by for the winter."

He sliced a piece of cornbread through the middle. "What you do after you got yer bread cut is you slather the bottom half with sweet pertater butter from the crock here—" He knifed some out of the jar and spread it. "—then you put the top half back on, and you got yerself a sweet little sammich."

ROSE PUSHED back from the table. "Luther, we busted up a still this morning in the Taterpatch. Know whose it might be?"

"There's a still up there?"

Bass finished off his buttermilk. "There was. We burned it."

"Musta been well hid. I never seen one up there."

Rose took out a matchstick and proceeded to work the end of it around his teeth. "There was a path worn in from the creek. We followed it back out, but where those fellas came out of the creek, we couldn't tell."

Luther scratched at the back of his hand. "Burned it, you say?"

"Yup."

"Well, someone's gonna squawk over that. I'll listen around. Quill, if I hear something, I get word to you."

"I hear it's the Crowes."

"I didn't know we had any Crowe families in this area of the county."

"We don't." Rose tucked his matchstick back in his shirt pocket. "They come up from below the state line. That's why I can't go after them."

"Do tell. You think they might rebuild?"

"Not if they're smart." Rose stood and carried his plate and jelly jar to the sink. "Mighty good meal, Luther. You want me to wash dishes?"

Luther brought his plate to the sink as well. "Nice of you to offer, but you an' yer friends got a long hike if you want to get back to Maryville before dark."

"Can't argue with that."

The group drifted out to the porch where Watson clamped onto Luther's hand. He gave it a firm shake. "It was good to get to know you, Mister Click."

"You, too, sir. You come back now. I don't get much company."

Bass latched onto Luther's hand next. "'Twas a mighty fine meal. I thank you."

"Yer kind to say so."

Watson and Bass went down the steps and set out for the road.

Rose held back. He put his arm around Luther's shoulders. "One thing," he said, gazing down at his cousin, "and I'm not complaining, you understand, but you ought to take a bath now and then. You're smelling a bit ripe."

Luther grinned. "Keeps the bears away."

"Come on."

"Quill Rose, I jump in the horse tank twice a year—spring an' fall. It's summer now, but if you think, I'll consider takin' a bath between times."

Rose gave the little man's shoulders a squeeze. "You take care," he said and went on down the steps after his companions.

"Give my best to Martha," Luther called out.

Rose waved a couple fingers in the air without swinging back.

Luther went inside and set about the business of putting up the extra food. He left out enough for a late supper, then washed and dried his dishes, after which he meandered outside to check his livestock and collect the eggs from the hens' hidden nests.

There was still good light when Luther finished, so he went on to his apple orchard. There he lifted the top on the first of his bee gums. An old-time bee man, Luther worked calmly and slowly, sometimes humming to the bees, sometimes talking to them, pulling up one honey frame and then another until he had examined them all. The bees appeared to ignore him. He couldn't remember the last time he had been stung.

Luther found the honey frames close to full. He decided the time had come to rob the gums of their rich flow of sweetness. Maybe in a couple days. First, he knew, he had to tend to his own still.

Chapter 2
The Stranger

LUTHER REMOVED the lid from the mash barrel. He laid it aside and studied the cap—the hard corn material that covered the mash. The thinness of it said the alcohol had been eating away at the underside of the cap.

Tomorrow, Luther figured, tomorrow it would be ready.

He cast his gaze around his still, making sure he had tidied everything up. Satisfied, he turned out the kerosene lamp that had provided the light by which he had worked.

In the darkness, Luther climbed the ladder to the ceiling. He pushed the trap door above him up, up enough that he could peer out without being seen. Fog diffused the morning sun, fog that limited his view to about twenty feet from the base of the rock bluff where he had buried his still.

Nothing moved.

Nothing out of place.

No prying eyes unless, Luther thought, they were behind a tree. If they were behind a tree, they couldn't see him if he couldn't see them.

Luther slid the sod-covered door aside and clambered out. When clear of the hole, he set the door back in place. After he kicked the forest litter around enough to hide the door's outline, Luther reached for the branch he had used as a drag the night before to obliterate his tracks coming in. He left, pulling the branch behind him, scratching out his shoe prints as he walked away. Luther stopped. He cocked his head to the side, listening for others who might be in the high mountain woods. He heard the call of a brown thrasher as complex as that of a catbird, but nothing more, so went on. However, some fifty yards on he stopped again. Listened again, and again went on.

A hundred yards down slope, Luther came to a stream where he used rocks as stepping stones to avoid making shoe prints in the soft soil of the bank. Once in the water, Luther poked his drag branch into a bush in such a way that it looked like it had fallen there, then he sloshed away.

He had a dozen different routes in and out of the woods that hid his still, and never traveled the same one twice in a month. Shiners who got caught, he knew, were the careless ones who walked the same routes to their stills until they had worn in paths that blind men could follow.

A mile downstream, at another rocky place, Luther scrambled out of the water and disappeared back into the woods. The fog had dissipated, and the sun made it a marvel of a morning in the mountains.

Luther, now so far from his still, no longer cared whether anyone saw him, so he walked with his head high down the face of the mountain toward the cove and home. He picked up a deer trail and, whistling, followed it out into a boulder pile that overlooked his farm a half-mile away.

A glint of light reflected up from something that laid to the side of one of the boulders. Luther stooped. He picked up two brass cartridges and rolled them through his fingers while he scanned the near horizon. Luther brought the cartridges to his nose—the odor of burnt gunpowder, still a bit strong.

Someone hunting deer?

Deer trailed this way before dawn on their way back to the deep woods after a night of foraging in the cove farmers' hayfields.

Luther went on out of the boulders, his eyes searching. Thirty yards on, he came on two large blood spores not yet dry, and boot prints, not hoof prints, and a felt hat. The boot prints jumbled up here and then turned, Luther saw, and retreated down the mountain toward a logging trail that crossed behind his buildings.

The marks in the forest litter told him that the owner of the boot prints was dragging the toe of his right boot. Luther picked up the hat and trotted along the trail.

The spots of blood in the leaves and grass came closer together the farther Luther traveled.

The trail went into another patch of rocks and there beyond it, at the base of a clump of gooseberry bushes, Luther found a man sprawled on his face—tan trousers tucked into high-topped leather boots, tan jacket, blood on the back and on the right sleeve.

Luther knelt beside him. He put his fingers on the man's neck, felt a pulse.

Faint.

Still a pulse.

He took a measure of the man and estimated he was no taller than himself, tho maybe a bit heavier, but not by much. Luther pulled up the man's jacket and shirt, to get at the wound, a hole the size of a quarter. He wadded his handkerchief into the wound in the man's shoulder. Next he rolled him over and stuffed a handkerchief from the man's jacket pocket into the hole in his upper chest.

Luther peered at the face—a stranger. A land agent or maybe a revenuer? Luther bent to going through the man's pockets for something that might tell him—a badge, a gun, or some papers. All he found were bits of lint and two silver dollars.

Luther shrugged himself out of his faded denim coat and his equally faded shirt. He ripped the lower half of the shirt away and into strips for bandages. One sleeve he tore off and tied it around the wound in the man's forearm. The rest of his shirt he wrapped around the man's chest and tied it, to hold the blood stoppers in place.

Luther's stringy muscles rippled as he worked. The morning air chilled him, enough that he pulled his coat back on and buttoned it up to his chin.

Done with what he could do, Luther stood. He hauled the man up by the front of his jacket, bent low and let the man's body flop over his shoulder. Luther, straining under the load, straightened again and plodded on down the slope, slipping on the grass.

At his house, he worked his way through the kitchen door with his burden still over his shoulder and went on inside, to the sleeping room. With his free hand, Luther pulled the feather tick back from his bed, then lowered the wounded man onto the straw mattress. He got rid of the man's boots and pulled the quilt back over him, to warm him.

The man, his face so pale, his breathing so shallow, Luther knew he needed a doctor, so he saddled one of his mules and rode out like the devil was after him.

Four miles on, the galloping mule near exhaustion, Luther saw what he had hoped for, a decade-old Cadillac parked in a grove of trees near a creek. He jumped from the saddle and let the mule trot on to the water while he ran to the car. Luther looked through the windshield at a man inside, stretched out on the front seat asleep, his legs hanging over the driver's door—the man, Doctor Alfred Schroeder.

Luther whipped open the passenger door. He shook Schroeder's shoulder. "Doc! Doc! I need you, Doc. Don't be drunk on me now."

Schroeder lifted an eyelid. "Luther? Luther Click?"

"Doc, I need you."

Schroeder twisted his head around to better see the man who had woke him. "Good God, Luther, I've been out all night delivering babies. Twins! Can't an honest man get some sleep?"

"Doc—"

"Don't Doc me. Get the hell out of here and close the damn door."

"Doc, a man's shot."

Schroeder yanked his legs into the car and rolled up on his rump. "Jesus K. Christ, why the hell didn't you say so?" He rubbed at the sand in his eyes. "Where is he?"

"My place."

"You shoot him?"

"Doc, I shoot varmints and an occasional deer for meat. I don't shoot people."

Schroeder slid himself over, behind the steering wheel. He pressed the starter button beneath the seat, firing up the engine. "Get in if you're going with me."

"What about my mule?"

"He's got grass, water and shade. That's better'n me. He's not going anywhere."

Luther had hardly gotten a foot in on the passenger side when Schroeder floored the gas pedal. He hauled himself the rest of the way inside as the car shot through the borrow ditch and bounced up onto the road.

"That blood on the back of your coat?" Schroeder asked, his eyes ahead.

"Probably. He was bleedin' pretty bad. I had to pack him off the mountain on my back."

"Oh, jeez, don't get blood on my car seat. Lean forward, wouldja?"

Luther turned. He braced an elbow into the seat back and a hand against the front panel to keep his back from touching the seat and keep himself from being thrown around as the car rocketed on at a speed that terrified him.

Schroeder yelled over the noise. "Who's the man?"

"Don't know. Never seen him before!"

"Got a wallet?"

"Nuthin'."

"Check all his pockets?"

"Yeah, kerchief. I stuffed that in his wound, and a couple silver dollars."

"You get the kerchief, I get the money. This time I get paid even if he dies on us!"

Chapter 3
Repair work

SCHROEDER SLID his car to a stop at the side of Luther's house. He bailed out, black bag in hand, and raced inside only to stagger back out, coughing. "God, man, the stench! Luther, what the hell have you been cooking in there?"

"Mutton and cabbage last night. It was good."

"Jesus, get all the doors and windows open and get some fresh air in there before that stench kills your man, if he's not already dead." Schroeder covered his mouth and nose with a handkerchief and pushed his way into the interior, through the kitchen and to the bedroom. He dropped his bag on a chair and stooped, listening to the man's breathing. "He's still going but, gawd, he's white. Must be a good two quarts low on the red stuff."

Schroeder peeled back the feather tick. He took out a pen knife and cut Luther's shirt bandage away. He lifted the blood-soaked handkerchief.

Blood oozed from the wound.

Luther peered over Schroeder's shoulder. "Bad, huh?"

"Look at the size of that hole. Wonder what the shooter was using?"

Luther fished in his pocket for a spent cartridge.

He found one and handed it to Schroeder who held it up to the light streaming through the window.

"Gawddamn, must be forty-caliber. People around here use that to bring down bear." He handed the shell back to Luther. "You say he's got a hole in his back?"

"Uh-huh. Bigger'n the one in front."

"Means the bullet passed through him front to back. Thank God for favors. I won't have to go digging around in him for the bullet. Luther?"

"Yessir?"

Schroeder probed around the wound site. "Boil me up some water so I can sterilize my instruments. And make us both some strong coffee."

"I kin do that, Doc."

"It's gonna take a while to clean him up."

LUTHER OPENED the bedroom window on his way out, then the windows and door in the front room. In the kitchen, he crumpled several pages of one of his New York Times and stuffed them and some dry kindling into the cookstove. After he set a match to it, he laid in a chunk of tinder-dry pine and several lengths of oak, the pine to make a hot fire quickly and the oak for a long, slow burn.

Fire started, Luther picked up a bucket from the sink and went out to the well. There he pumped the bucket full of fresh water.

The pump was one of Luther's few concessions to modern times. He had grown up cranking the windlass to lower and raise the bucket in his father's hand-dug well. That was work.

Several years ago, a traveling salesman came through the cove, demonstrating hand pumps that could be installed in wells. Not only could you get water up fast, the drummer said, you could also cover the well so leaves and dirt would no longer blow in.

The advantages of a cover appealed to Luther. At least once a year, a stray cat or a possum got curious and fell in the well and drowned. If he didn't find it right away and get it out, the critter spoiled in the water. Then Luther had to bucket all the water out of the well and go down on the rope to scrub the walls clean—a hard, time-consuming job.

So he bought a pump and the piping on the spot, installed it and a cover he made, and the pump had worked like a sweetheart ever since.

Luther poured his coffeepot half full from his bucket and put both the pot and the bucket on the stove to boil. The pot got two handfuls of ground beans before Luther went back to the bedroom where he found Schroeder examining the man's arm.

"See this?" Schroeder said.

Luther leaned in and followed Schroeder's probe. "You sterilize that, Doc?"

"Yes, in alcohol I chose not to drink. See these bone chips here?"

"Uh-huh."

"The bullet shattered the ulna—this long bone— tore up the muscle, too, but it missed the ulnar artery and the vein that go along there, so the bleeding's almost stopped. He would have bled to death if the ulnar had been compromised."

Luther scratched at the side of his face. "What do

you got to do?"

"Well, I'm going to try to find all the big pieces of the ulna, fit them back together." Schroeder continued probing through the wound, laying some of the torn muscle aside. "The chips and small splinters, I'll just have to throw away. I can't have them floating around in there. Then I'll clean the wound, disinfect it, wrap it tight, splint the arm and pray to God he doesn't get an infection."

"You can save the arm, then?"

Schroeder straightened up. He rolled his shoulder, working out the tension. "Won't be as strong as it was. Luther, to make it work, I need two boards about three inches wide and the length of your lower arm for the splint. You got something like that?"

"I can cut 'em."

"You do that." Schroeder bent over the wound again. "For now, I'm going to close that arm up and take a nap. You wake me when the splint's ready and the water's boiling, but not before."

Luther went out to his carpentry shop next to his barn. He took down an oak plank, some sixteen inches wide and sighted down the length of it, to make sure it was straight, then cut off a ten-inch length with his crosscut saw.

He pencil marked two three-inch widths, took down his ripping saw, and cut them away from the short length of plank.

Luther examined the splints. Rough edges. He didn't like that, so he got out a block plane and smoothed and rounded the edges until there were no splinters to catch at fingers or bandages.

Splints in hand, he hiked to the house and into the kitchen where he heard both the water and the coffee boiling. Luther took down two stoneware cups from his dishes shelf. He filled them with coffee and went on to the bedroom where he set a cup on a stack of Colliers magazines. Luther touched Schroeder's shoulder. "Doc?"

"Mmmm?"

"Coffee's ready. So's the hot water and the splints." He put a cup in Schroeder open hand.

Schroeder closed his hand around the cup. "Feels good. Smells good, too." He sipped at the black liquid. "Ohmigod!"

"Strong enough?"

"I may never sleep again." Schroeder huffed on his coffee, then took a second sip. "Whoooeeh, that's powerful."

"The splints," Luther said, holding them out.

Schroeder ran his hands over them. He looked up, his eyes warm with admiration. "Luther, these are really good, really smooth."

"I planed 'em. Didn't want no splinters."

"Beautiful." Schroeder set the splints aside as he hoisted himself out of the chair. He picked up his instrument bag. "Let's go boil my tools and get to work."

SCHROEDER HELD his hands above the bucket of boiling water. "This is the part I hate."

He plunged them in, yelped and yanked them out. "Damn, there's gotta be a better way for a doc to sterilize his hands, one that doesn't scald your skin."

Trembling from his dip in the super-hot water, Schroeder gathered up the plate of sterilized instruments and hurried to the bedroom. There he uncovered the chest wound. "Luther, light a lamp, would you? Hold it over my shoulder. I need to see what I'm doing."

Luther carried over a kerosene lamp from a side table. He turned up the wick, lit it, and adjusted the wick until he had a yellow-white flame. Luther held the lamp over Schroeder's shoulder.

Schroeder eased his probe and forceps down into the hole and pressed muscle away from a rib. "This fellow's led a righteous life. Luther, see here? See how the bullet went right between the ribs, chipped 'em a bit, but that's all. If that chunk of lead had hit the rib square, it would have shattered it and sent bone shards into the lung."

"Been a mess, huh?"

"We'd have had hell to pay. But as it is, all we've got to do is close the wound, swab some iodine over it, stitch the wound shut, and bandage it." Schroeder pulled his forceps out of the wound. He aimed it at Luther. "In the boiling water out in the kitchen is my sewing needle. Get it for me. And bring that table up on the other side of the bed for the lamp. I need that light."

Luther moved the table. He pushed aside the National Geographics he kept on it and set the lamp in the open space while Schroeder went back to probing in the wound, checking for surprises that might be tucked away in the damaged muscle.

Luther returned with a needle clamped in a forceps.

Schroeder pulled a hank of thread from a bottle that kept the thread sterile. He slipped the thread through the needle's eye and tied the ends off.

"You hold that for me," he said and went to unscrewing the cap on his iodine bottle. With the thumb and forefinger of one hand, he squeezed the wound shut. With his other hand, he dabbed iodine over the edges of the wound, took the needle from Luther's forceps and went to stitching—piercing the skin and push/pulling the needle and thread through. Loop after loop, seven in all. He tied the last stitch off and snipped the thread.

Schroeder laid his instruments on the plate and handed the plate to Luther. "Clean them up, and we'll do his back."

Luther disappeared.

Schroeder busied himself, positioning a sterile pad over the wound. He taped it in place, then rolled the man onto his stomach.

With his pen knife, Schroeder cut the man's jacket and shirt away. When he could get to the wound, he lifted the bloody handkerchief Luther had stuffed in the shoulder. Schroeder took another sterile pad from his instrument bag.

Luther returned with the freshly sterilized instruments.

Schroeder helped himself to the probe. "Just what I need."

With one hand, he dabbed at the blood coming out of the wound while, with the other, he probed the wound to see the damage. "Mmm-mmuh, blew a hole in the shoulder blade. No surprise at that, but I can't see what damage may have been done to the rib behind it. The bone fragments should have been blown out. Oops."

Luther crowded in for a look.

"See here? A bone fragment caught in the muscle. I need my small forceps." Schroeder found it on the plate. Working with both the probe and the small forceps, he removed one bit of bone after another—six in all—dropped them on the plate. Schroeder leaned down to the wound. He listened. "No air coming out. The bullet missed the lung."

Schroeder traded his probe for a scalpel and, with great care, sliced away ragged bits of muscle and skin. He cleaned the wound and closed it with rapid stitching.

"That's the worst," Schroeder said as he tied off the final stitch and cut the thread. "If he gets pneumonia and goes to coughing, Luther, he'll tear those stitches out and all my handiwork will have been for nothing. We've got to keep him from getting pneumonia."

"I'll look after him."

"I know you will." Schroeder rummaged in his instrument bag for a third sterile pad. He found it and covered the wound. Schroeder mopped the sweat from his forehead with his shirt sleeve before he taped the pad in place. "How long we been at it, Luther"

"An hour I'd guess."

"Your mattress is soaked in patches. We can't leave this fella laying in wet blood. You got another?"

"Hanging in my shop."

"Get it while I wash up." Schroeder wiggled his bloody fingers for Luther to see. "I'll boil my instruments, too, so we can go to work on that arm."

Schroeder, stiff from standing so long, moved toward the kitchen like a man whose knees were locked.

LUTHER RETURNED with the spare mattress and found Schroeder in the bedroom, pacing, a cup of coffee in his hand.

Schroeder set his cup by the lamp. "Let's be at it. You roll our man into my arms. When I pick him up, you get that filthy mattress off and float the new one on. After we get him resettled, Luther, my man, you're going to be my assistant surgeon as we work on the arm."

LUTHER DABBED the blood away from the wound as Schroeder probed for the last fragment of bone. He found it and extracted it with the greatest of care. "Fifteen, Luther, fifteen in all."

"What do we do next?"

Schroeder sorted through the fragments he'd dropped in a dish. "Have you ever done one of those jigsaw puzzles?"

"My bother sent me one."

"We're gonna put as many of these bits and pieces back in with the bone that will fit. That done, we'll close the muscle over them, sew it all up, and hope the bone knits back together."

Luther dropped his swab in a bucket. "You ever done this?"

"I've only read about it." Schroeder picked up a jagged bit of bone with his forceps. He held it up to the light and studied its edges. "I'd say this one fits right up against the upper part of the ulna here."

He worked the piece into place. Sweating, Schroeder knuckled a dribble out of his eye.

SCHROEDER FLOPPED onto a chair, haggard, blood smears on the front of his shirt where he'd wiped his fingers. "Damn, how long have we been at this?"

Luther glanced up at his mantle clock as he laid the man's wrapped and splinted arm at his side. "Four hours, I'd say." He pulled the feather tick over the man, snugged it up around his shoulders.

"If that bone doesn't grow back together, Luther, some damn surgeon's going to saw his arm off below the elbow. A simple fracture is easy, you know. Fall off the back steps and break your leg, I can fix that in my sleep. But bullet wounds like this one, this is damn tricky stuff."

Luther collected the surgery instruments. "What do I do to take care of him?"

"Not much until he wakes up. That could be a day or two. Sleep's the best healer." Schroeder yawned a lion-sized yawn. "I'll come by to change his bandages every day and make sure he's not getting any infection."

"You want me to clean up your tools, Doc?"

"That would be kind of you. Boil them good, then I'll pack them back in my bag."

Luther picked up the plate and the bucket of bloody bandages and pads, and carried everything into the kitchen. He stuffed the bandages and pads into the stove to burn and set about washing the few surgery instruments that Schroeder carried with him. When he had them clean, he dropped them in the bucket of boiling water. Luther glanced up to see Schroeder leaning against the door frame.

"Wouldn't happen to have something to eat, would you, Luther?"

Luther fished up each instrument from the water with a long forceps and placed it on a clean plate. "Got mutton and cabbage. 'Course it's cold. And an apple pie Missus Anderson sent home with me."

"Any bread?"

"Good bread. Baked it two nights ago."

"Tell you what, I'll slice up that hunk of sheep you've got, and we can make us a couple mutton and cabbage sandwiches."

"And cheese. I got me some of Mister Anderson's cheddar cheese that he makes. It's all out in the spring house, keeping cold. I'll get it. Bread's in a box there." Luther pointed to the shelf. "You can cut it."

Schroeder packed his instruments and put his black bag by the back door. Then he got down plates and the bread box. Schroeder pawed through Luther's collection of knifes for a sharp one, gave up the search and went to his bag for a scalpel. With it, he sliced the bread, one narrow cut after another.

Luther elbowed his way through the doorway with a tray of bowls and a pie pan. A lard bucket swung by its bail from his arm. "Buttermilk," Luther said when

Schroeder looked at it.

AFTER THE MEAL, Luther lifted a slab of apple pie onto Schroeder's plate and placed a slice of cheese on it. "Yankees have their pie this way, I've read."

Schroeder tried it. "Cheese on pie, never would have thought of that." He leaned his fork on his plate. "Wonder why they didn't kill him?"

Luther sat down with his own slab of pie and cheese. "Who?"

"Your man in there." Schroeder gave a jerk of his head toward the bedroom.

"Knocked him down with two bullets. Probably figured he'd bleed to death, so why waste a third." Luther scooped a bite into his mouth and worked the pie around his molars.

"Who the hell could he be?"

"Those logger boots of his say he's a land agent, but my nose—" Luther tapped the side of his nose with his fork. "—my nose says he's a tax man."

"Federal?"

"Sure not local."

"After your still?"

Luther went back at his pie. "Doubt it. Probably after a neighbor who talked too much or got careless. There's some mean people up this way who think nuthin' of shootin' a man from ambush."

Schroeder belched. He pounded his chest. "It's the cabbage, Luther. Sure-fire gas maker. Well, one thing's certain, I've got to tell the sheriff about this. This going to cause trouble for you?"

"No. Quill Rose and me, we're shirttail relatives. I even help turn out the vote for him."

"You? A hoochmaker?"

Luther winked at Schroeder. "He don't know that. Thinks the trade went to the grave with my daddy, and I'm not about to disabuse him of his belief."

Schroeder shook his shaggy mane. "I don't know how you do it, Luther."

"I'm small fish, and I'm careful."

"Well, I better look in on my patient, then get on my way." Schroeder pushed his chair back and stood. "Oh, if your mule's still at the creek, I'll slap him on the rump if you think he'll come home."

"He'll come home. But Jake's like me, not much in a hurry if he don't have a driver."

LUTHER, ALONE, put the food that needed to be kept cold in the spring house, and washed his dishes and cleaned the kitchen. Those chores done, he settled on a chair in the bedroom and took up watch over his silent company. The man breathed more easily now.

The pain, Luther thought, must not be as severe as it was.

With nothing better to do, he picked up an issue of the Geographic and thumbed through the pages. He stopped on an article he had been meaning to read, about a cannibal tribe in Borneo. Luther turned to the map page and located the island. He had forgotten it was near Australia.

He read with interest. The rich descriptions of the mountains and the lush jungle growth transported him out of the cove.

He read through the remainder of afternoon and into the evening, read until he sensed a pair of eyes on him. Luther looked over—the man was still asleep. Then he heard a blowing at the window.

Luther twisted around and found himself nose to muzzle with Jake, the mule's long face and ears inside the open window.

The mule shook his bridle.

Luther stroked the bridge of the mule's muzzle, then pushed him back and climbed out the window after him.

Outside, he led Jake to the barn, took off his saddle and bridle, and shook out some hay in the corner of a stall. He fed his other mule and what little livestock he had, then went back to the house by way of the spring house where he gathered up the last of the pie and buttermilk and a chunk of cheese for supper.

He ate at the table as he always did, and, when finished, feeling the first cool night breeze, he strolled from room to room, closing windows and doors. After he finished in the bedroom, he sat in his chair and resumed his watch.

Luther couldn't stop himself. He picked up a Harper's Magazine and soon fell into chortling as he read through a short piece, *A Sock in the Jaw – French Style*, by a writer he had never read before, a young man from Columbus, Ohio, the editor's note said, by the name of James Thurber.

Luther read into the night, hour after hour, until his eyes lids lost their tension and drooped, slid closed. The lamp sputtered and winked out, out of kerosene.

Chapter 4
Quill Rose returns

LUTHER WOKE with a God-awful crick in his neck and drool down the front of his shirt. He rubbed at his neck, kneading and massaging the muscles, trying to get the crick to release.

Before him laid his unexpected house guest still in a deep sleep. Luther pressed his hand to the man's forehead. Warm. Should be, all covered up like this.

He left him and went to the kitchen, to start a fire in the cookstove so he could boil coffee and fry an egg.

A car roared up into his yard. Luther heard a door slam as he wiped his hands dry on his trousers.

Schroeder came hustling through the kitchen door. "How's the patient?"

Luther rubbed at his elbow. "No change near as I can tell."

"Well, I'll just check him over. Give me a hand changing the dressings?"

"Glad to."

Luther followed Schroeder to the bedroom. There he leaned against the door jamb and watched the mountain medic put his fingertips on the man's wrist.

"Pulse seems a bit stronger." Schroeder laid his hand on the man's forehead. "No fever. That's good. Luther, let's get at the bandages, see if he's leaking any."

Luther stripped the feather tick away. With care, he and Schroeder rolled the man up on his side—his left side. Luther steadied him, and Schroeder peeled away the adhesive tape that held a swatch bandage against the right shoulder blade.

Schroeder lifted the bandage back. Stitches showed the work he had done to close the bullet hole, blood clotted around the needlework.

Schroeder ran his fingers over the stitches, over the clotting. He studied his fingertips. "Still got some oozing."

He rummaged in his medicine bag.

"Whatcha lookin' for, Doc?"

"A sterile bandage. Ahh, here we are." Schroeder brought out a paper-wrapped packet and tore it open. He laid the fresh gauze pad over the wound. With Luther holding the pad in place, he taped it down.

Luther rolled the man back onto his back.

Schroeder peeled off the chest bandage and touched the clots. "Yes, yes, this one I like. It's dry. New bandage, please."

Luther found another paper-wrapped packet in Schroeder's medicine bag. He held the packet out. "You gonna do the arm, too?"

"That's the worst. We've got to get it aired out." He untied the splints and unwrapped the arm. "Oh, God."

Luther leaned over Schroeder's shoulder. "What is it?"

"We've got swelling here, and the wound's oozing." Schroeder went about swabbing the wound clean. He tossed the bloody pad in a waste bucket at the side of the bed, then rewrapped the arm with a clean bandage, this time more loosely before he resplinted it.

Schroeder packed his black bag. "That's about all I can do for him. Luther, when he wakes up, I want you to get a lot of water in him. He's going to be dry."

"When you think that might be?"

"Today, tomorrow, could be next week."

Schroeder hurried out the door. He flung himself in his car and tromped on the accelerator.

Luther watched him rocket out of the yard. Alone again, he went to the barn, the barn smelling of livestock and dry hay, and turned his mules out to pasture. He also fed his lone sow and spread corn for his chickens. Luther knew where the biddies hid their nests, so he made the rounds of the weeds, gathering eggs—six, not a bad day's production from eight hens.

He checked on the wounded man still in a deep sleep and went on to his garden. There he sharpened his hoe with a whetstone and went about chopping out the velvetleaf and pigweed that had gotten a start on him while his attention had been elsewhere.

At noon, Luther pulled a handful of carrots and onions and picked a handful of lambs quarter leaves and two tomatoes that had turned a deep, rich red. He washed them and chopped them and dumped them in a pot to stew with the last of a pork roast he had been saving for stew. He thought about cooking the stew fast at a high boil, but decided against it. Instead, he put the pot on the back of the cookstove to simmer for supper.

For noon dinner, he picked another tomato and ate it fresh with cheese. Luther didn't need much to keep him going. He'd never been a big eater, not even as a boy. But he did eat when he had company. He liked that—company.

Luther checked again on his patient. He washed the man's face with cool well water, then took his soap mug down from the shelf where he kept his shaving gear. Luther worked up a lather and brushed it over the man's cheeks, chin, and throat. Next he took down his straight razor and scraped away the man's growth of beard.

That done, Luther peered at his own reflection in his shaving mirror and decided a shave for himself wouldn't hurt. So he lathered up and laid the blade to his face.

Most men shaved every day out of habit. Luther shaved when he thought about it, which might be once a week or, in the winter, not at all. At those times, if he failed to get a haircut, all people saw of his face were two eyes and a nose peeking out through a salt-and-pepper bush.

Luther sloshed his razor clean and pronounced himself good for another week.

For the afternoon, he hoisted his hoe to his shoulder and strolled out to his cornfield, the air dry, smelling of dust. For the most part he chopped weeds, but every now and then, he checked the pods on the half-runner beans that twined up the corn stalks. He could feel that they were filling out. He'd have to pick in the next day or two.

At the far end of the field, he snapped off two muskmelons in his melon patch and walked out of the field, humming an aimless tune.

"Understand you got company," a voice said and an

arm slipped around his shoulders.

Luther jumped.

He dropped his hoe and almost lost the melons.

He turned, shaking. "Gawdamighty, Quill Rose, you scare a man to death sneaking up on him like that."

Rose laughed. "Next time, cousin, I'll whistle and throw rocks so you know I'm coming. Who's at your house?"

"Don't know, Quill."

"He still out of it?"

"Hasn't opened an eye since I packed him off the mountain."

"Doc says he owes his life to you."

"To God, maybe. I just happened by."

"Well, let's see if I recognize him."

"Think you might?"

"Never know." Rose reached for the melons. "Want me to carry these? You almost dropped them back there."

"Least you can do to be helpful."

Luther transferred his load, and the two walked on, up the lane toward the house, chattering, Rose's suit coat flapping in the breeze.

"Stay for supper?" Luther asked after he put the melons in the sink.

"Maybe even the night if you can put me up."

Luther waved a hand toward the stew pot on the stove. "Lift the cover. Tell me what you think of it."

Quill Rose picked up the cover. He inhaled the aroma, dipped a finger into the simmering mass and sucked the juice off. "I taste oregano—just a hint—and maybe a little tarragon? Mmmm."

"Only you would know, Quill. People around here, all they know about flavorings is black pepper and salt."

"That's all I knew until I got married. You know Martha, best cook in Maryville."

"Don't show on you."

Rose chuckled. "No, it surely don't. Where's your guest?"

"Sleepin' room."

The two went into the bedroom. There Luther slipped into the chair by the bed. He leaned forward and put his hand on the man's forehead. "Temperature's all right, breathing's fine. I just wisht to God he'd wake up. Doc says he's gonna dry out if we don't get some water in him soon. He worries me, Quill."

"And you don't know who he is?"

"No, never seen him afore."

"Wouldn't expect you had. This is his first time in."

"You know him?"

"Eamon McCool, federal tax man from Johnson City. Treasury sent him in to catch moonshiners. Hell of a reputation up in northeast Tennessee. He was in my office last week, telling me what his job was."

"Oh. You're thinkin' somebody up this way must have caught onto him?"

"That's my guess."

"Strangers do tend to stick out, like folks wavin' bed sheets. Quill, we got some mean boys back in these hills, boys that don't like strangers."

"That's why I don't come around unless I have to." Rose worried the bed post with the toe of his boot.

"Now I have to."

"Alone?"

"You don't catch anybody or nothing with a posse, Luther, not even a cold."

"I s'pose you want me to show you where I found him."

"That's where I start."

Luther grubbed in his bib pocket. He produced two empty cartridges. "You'll be wantin' these."

"Doc said you had them." Rose examined the end of the brasses. He pointed to one. "See this mark? Made by a different kind of firing pin. Likely a German Mauser. Lots of them came back from the war. Trophies, you know. This could be helpful."

He jingled the shells in his hand while he and Luther went on out and up the logging trail toward Gobbler's Knob.

Twenty minutes of climbing brought them to the bloody patch of ground where Luther had found McCool. There, beyond, was the jumble of boulders where he had found the shells.

"You came from up there?" Rose asked, gesturing further up the mountain.

Luther nodded.

"If you don't mind me asking, what were you doing up there?"

"Got a couple ginseng beds in the trees on the other side, near the top. I was checkin' on them. Don't want poachers finding them."

"Ginseng beds and not a still? I know you've got one."

Luther shrugged.

Rose did, too, and went to the boulders and beyond. He came to an area of soft ground and there saw the prints of Luther's shoes coming down the mountain. Rose circled to the side, scanning the ground as he went. He stopped. "Luther, look at this. Boot prints. Two sets. They go into the boulders that way, and they come back out by the same route."

Spreading his hands and arms, Rose measured the spacing between the boot prints leaving the boulders. "They were running when they left. Pretty good-sized fellas by the size of the prints. And look at this—" Rose dropped to one knee. He worked a finger around one of the prints. "See here? Somehow the corner of the inside of the heel is broke off. That's going to hang him if McCool dies because nobody around here throws his boots away."

Luther massaged his chin as he, too, studied the prints. "That's some good detective work, my friend."

"Just good eyesight. You better go home and see how your guest is doing. I'll follow these boys to see where they went."

Luther started down the mountain, but turned back. "Comin' in for supper?"

"About dark, maybe."

"I'll keep the stew hot."

SUNDOWN CAME and sundown went. Luther lit lamps in the sleeping room and the kitchen, and stoked the fire in the stove to keep the stew warm. With nothing more to do, he picked up a book, *Streets of the Night*, a novel his brother had sent him.

He opened it and read a scribbled note on the fly leaf: *Bill, a gift in appreciation of the friendship we share. Dos.* He turned to page one and read into the night, dozing off somewhere in the third chapter.

LUTHER WOKE to the click of a spoon against a dish. He cast a glazed eye at the clock on the mantle: eleven forty.

Luther muscled himself out of his chair. He stretched and shook himself and wandered into the kitchen where he found Quill Rose at the table, scooping stew into his mouth. "Where you been?" he asked.

Rose mopped his lips with his sleeve. "Other side of the mountain. You were asleep. I didn't want to wake you. Good stew, by the way."

"I'll get some an' join you." Luther filled a bowl and set out a half-loaf of bread. "You want butter? I can get it from the spring house."

"No, I'm fine without it." Rose tore a chunk off the half-loaf and soaked it in his stew.

Luther poured coffee for the two. "Ever been to Boston?"

"Luther, I've never been out of the county except to Knoxville a couple times."

Luther sat down. "I've not even been to Knoxville, but I've been readin' about Boston in this book. Sounds like an interesting place." He pushed the book across the table to Rose.

Rose gazed at the cover. "John Dos Passos. Who's he?"

"Somebody my brother knows. Find anything interesting out there?"

"A still, about two miles from the shooting. It's in a grove of trees by a stream way back the other side of the mountain. Wouldn't find it unless you were looking for it."

"Anyone there?"

"Deserted. I checked the mash. Somebody'll be coming back in a day or two to do some work. How's our man?"

Luther chewed on a piece of the roast. "Gettin' restless. He's startin' to move some, moans a bit. Wisht he'd wake up."

"Maybe getting ready to."

"Quill, I surely hope so. Want some melon? I got it cut."

Rose grinned, his cheeks like a chipmunk's, packed with bread and stew. "You know where my heart is."

They ate until there was no more stew or bread or melon. Filled at last, Quill Rose stretched out on a mat in the front room and fell asleep before Luther could get a blanket for him. For himself, Luther went back to the bedroom. He turned out the lamp and resumed his watch by moonlight. He stretched and yawned and settled in his chair and was himself soon asleep.

Chapter 5
Renegades

A TUGGING at his pant leg and someone whispering his name woke Luther. "Wha–"

"Shhh. Shhh."

He peered down at a dark form by his feet. "Quill?"

"Quiet. You've got company."

"Huh?"

"The window. Look."

Luther did. Shapes passed by, outlined by the moonlight. One came toward the window, closer and closer until the silhouette of a head and wide-brimmed hat pressed against the glass.

Quill Rose rolled. He grabbed the chamber pot from under the bed and hurled it at the form, shattering the window. The silhouette swore.

Rose scrambled to his feet. He ran from the room before Luther could get out of his chair. The kitchen door banged open, and Luther heard Rose yell "Stop!" and the crack of a revolver from a distance.

A gun at the corner of the house barked.

A second revolver shot answered. A bullet smashed through the upper half of the window and thunked into the wall above Luther's head.

He dove for the floor.

The gun at the corner of the house barked a

second and third time and a burst of revolver shots answered, bullets thunking into the outside wall.

The near gun barked three times in rapid succession, followed by the click of metal on metal.

"He's outta ammunition, Earl," a voice in the distance called out. "We kin kill him."

"Not if he reloads," a second voice answered. "Let's get ta hell outta here."

Then Luther heard the pounding of feet, running from the corner of his house, down the side yard toward the road.

He eased himself up to his knees. From there he fumbled for matches on a side table, found one, and snapped it with the tip of his thumbnail. The flame it released illuminated the room, the light glinting off shards of glass scattered about the floor and more shards in the window frame.

Luther lit the lamp and checked McCool, apparently undisturbed by the gunfight.

Luther went about collecting a hammer, a handful of tacks, and a blanket, the blanket to nail across the top of the window frame. He stepped up on a chair and drove the first tack in.

Quill Rose walked in on him, Rose clutching a long-barreled Colt forty-five.

Luther glanced down. "They get away?"

"Yeah. Had mules down by your cornfield. They got to them before I could run 'em down. Rode off fast."

"Any idea who they might be?"

"Oh, yeah." Rose opened his revolver's cylinder. He shook out the empty shells. "That one the fella called

Earl, that's Earl Fennimore. I've had him in jail, so I know his voice. That being Earl makes the other one his cousin, Bobby Ray Reilly. I've had him in jail, too."

Luther hammered in another tack. "Goin' after 'em?"

"Not tonight." Rose took out a fistful of bullets and, with deliberation, pressed a new cartridge in each chamber. "No, not when I'm expected. That's what gets lawmen killed. I'll get them when I've got the advantage."

Luther shambled out to the kitchen and returned with a broom. "Help me sweep up this glass?"

Rose spun the loaded cylinder. Satisfied, he snapped it shut and laid the mammoth weapon on the bed.

Luther tipped his head toward a newspaper on the night stand. "If you'll get that and hold it down here, I'll sweep the glass onto it."

Rose helped himself to the newspaper—the New York Times—and crouched down. "You knew those boys were shiners."

Luther swept, herding the shards toward the paper Rose held in place. "Heard talk, but never knew where their still was. I avoid 'em and we get along."

"They didn't avoid you tonight."

"No. That's a might worrisome." Luther swept the glass onto the paper.

"Worrisome, yes, but not for the rest of the night."

"How do you figure?"

"Those two are gonna run deep into the hills. There are places back there to get lost in."

"So my daddy always said."

———

THE LAST HOUR before dawn, Quill Rose sat outside on the back step, cleaning his revolver while he watched the mountain, not wanting to be surprised a second time. He didn't surrender to sleep until the sun had slipped through the notch between Gobbler's Knob and the Cherokee Maid, the next mountain to the south.

LUTHER SAW Rose there, his back against the doorjamb, arms folded before him, gun in hand, head slumped forward on his chest. He stepped through the doorway without so much as making a board creak and went through the backyard to the barn, to do morning chores.

Luther stopped at the smokehouse after he had gathered the eggs his chickens had laid the day before. He cut two slabs from a ham for breakfast, picked up the last of his supply of fresh milk from the spring house and, slipping by the sleeping Quill Rose, set about putting together something good in the kitchen.

He started by whipping up a batter for cathead biscuits, and, while they baked in the cookstove's oven, fried the hamsteaks and eggs. When ready, Luther shoveled them out of the skillet and made red-eye gravy with the drippings. The aroma, mouth-watering.

He filled a plate for himself and took it and a cup of coffee outside and sat down on the step next to Rose.

Rose opened his eyes.

Luther aimed his fork at the slab of ham. "Figured the good smells would bring you 'round."

"Surely do, don't they?" Rose stretched. He shook himself awake before he slid the big gun into the holster that hung from his shoulder.

Luther gave a head jerk toward the door. "Your plate's in the warmin' box over the stove. You kin pour your own coffee."

Seemingly it took only a moment and Rose returned, smiling over his plate mounded up. "Biscuits and gravy, ham and eggs, this is good eating, Luther."

"Figured I better fill your belly before you go after Earl and Bobby Ray. It could be a long time afore you get to eat again."

Rose gazed around as he packed in the food, noting Luther's apple trees, the great lilac bushes that sheltered the outhouse, the garden, his cornfield and the pasture where the mules lazed. "You really got it nice here," he said.

"I like it."

"You know, Luther, if I don't die in office, I'd like to have me a little farm like this. What you don't grow for food, you can shoot in the woods or catch in a stream or pick wild. You can't do that in Maryville."

Luther cut another bite from his hamsteak. "No, I don't 'spect you kin."

"The town's grown up too much. Did you know we've got almost five hundred people in Maryville now? And we've got the college. It's almost more civilization than a body can stand."

Luther stared at Rose's empty plate. "How'd you

put that down so fast?"

"Afraid I was a tad hungry."

"More biscuits and gravy?"

Rose's long face lifted in a smile. "Thought you'd never ask."

"Help yourself. You know where it 'tis."

Rose pulled himself to his feet. He went into the kitchen and came back, sopping a biscuit in his plate filled with gravy. "Awfully good. But I better get back in the mountains and catch my boys."

"I'll pack you some food."

"Not necessary."

"I got sammiches made up. How about you set a spell longer?" Luther disappeared into the kitchen where he found a cloth. He spread it on the table and proceeded to stack sandwiches, a ripe tomato, and a fried pie on the cloth. He bundled them and tied a knot at the top that Rose could use for a handle. When he came back out, Luther traded the bundle for Rose's empty plate.

Rose hefted the food. "With all this, I might not come back for a week."

IT TOOK him the better part of two hours to get to the neighborhood of the still. Rose circled around to the downwind side, so not even his scent would carry to the still, then he eased up on it. He stopped some distance out and dropped to his knees. He listened—no sound other than the rustle of mountain grass and the to-to-to-tooo call of a waterthrush—nor did he see any movement.

Rose left his food bundle and hat and crawled forward to the edge of the trees that hid the still from casual sight. He pulled his long-barreled revolver from its holster and crept from tree trunk to tree trunk until the still laid before him.

Nothing.

No one.

Rose pored over the ground, checking for signs that the owners had returned and gone since he was last there.

Still nothing.

Nothing disturbed.

Not a new boot print anywhere.

Rose snapped a branch from a silver dogwood and with it swept away his boot prints. In the meadow, as he retreated, he combed up the grass that he had bent down on his crawl in. He picked up his bundle and hat and swung further to the east until he came to the creek that flowed past the still.

He stepped into the water and splashed upstream to high ground well beyond the still. There Rose stopped. He ate a sandwich and drank his fill of water, and climbed up a bluff that overlooked all approaches. He found a pocket in the bluff and slipped into it, sure no one who might come down from above would see him, a pocket that gave him a view of the trees that hid the still.

Rose settled in.

Hours passed.

Late in the afternoon, motion in the sky caught his attention. Quill Rose shaded his eyes with his hat, straining, and saw five large birds wheeling, turning in the air, circling over a point a distance below him.

Turkey vultures.

One drifted lower and dropped into the meadow grass. A second and a third slid out of the sky and disappeared into the grass as well. Numbers four and five continued wheeling in circles, and then they, too, swooped down.

Gotta be something dead down there. Earl? I could have winged him.

More turkey vultures drifted into the area—three, four, a dozen. Rose counted them.

Word's getting around.

He tucked his cache of food into a crevice in the back of the pocket and eased his way out and off the bluff. Cautious about leaving a trail, Rose made his way to the creek and followed it down to as close as he could get to where the vultures had landed.

He trekked his way up into the meadow and stopped.

Rose cocked his head to the side and heard the birds gabbling and quarreling.

He broke into a trot that carried him down on them. The near birds flapped their way up into the air and winged off, but the others continued to peck and pull at whatever they had found in the grass.

Rose saw shoes and trouser legs. He charged on the birds, whooping and waving his arms. All but one took to their wings.

That one wheeled on Rose.

Rose ran at him, but the vulture came up with his talons and beat its wings at Rose, all the time keeping itself between the intruder and the body in the grass.

Rose circled, and the bird flapped and danced in the same direction.

Rose ran on the bird again, and the bird raked him with its talons. Angered, Rose whipped out his revolver and fired.

The bird fell to the ground, dead.

He kicked it out of the way, the better to see the body twisted in the grass. Rose's stomach churned, and he wretched. Most of the man's face and the flesh of his hands had been eaten away.

Rose forced himself to examine the bloody skull. He found a hole in the forehead and, when he rolled the man over, most of the back of the head was gone, blown away by the bullet that had killed him.

Drained of strength and emotion, Rose dragged himself to the still, caring not whether he left a trail. He remembered having seen a shovel there. He needed that shovel now. He found it and carried it back.

Two vultures had returned and were picking at the head when Rose came up. He ran at them, waving the shovel, and knocked both birds down when they tried to take to the air. He swung the shovel like a blade and severed the head of first one vulture and then the other. Then he emptied his revolver at those that soared above him.

The racket of the gun shots drove them away.

Quill Rose collapsed among the carrion.

After a time, he roused himself and forced himself to go through the man's pockets.

Nothing.

Nothing to tell who the man was, and with so little of his face left—

Rose drove the shovel into the sod. He dug and pitched until he struck stone. He lengthened the hole to the size of a grave and pulled the man in by his heels. Rose positioned the arms at the side of the body and, with his hands, raked the dirt into the hole. He recovered the shovel and used it to mound the remaining soil and sod over the grave so the soil would settle to level as the body decomposed and the bones collapsed.

Whoever you might be, in time, only the mountain will remember you were buried here, Rose thought.

He dug a hole for the vultures. Rose threw them in and covered them, and, in anger, swung the shovel like an athlete would a hammer. He let it go, flinging it as far as he could, heard it thwack into the grass some distance away.

Rose's anger became rage, but he forced himself to rein it back. He had to control it. Senseless killings—

He stalked away, back up the mountain to the bluff, to the hole in the rock wall and resumed his watch. He cleaned his gun, and his rage subsided. He reloaded his revolver and placed it on a rock in front of him and settled back to wait.

The sun drifted below the rounded peak of Gobbler's Knob. The twilight that enveloped Quill Rose's side of the mountain turned progressively to deeper and deeper shades of purple, then to black. The night stars winked on one at a time, in handfuls, and finally in masses.

Rose turned his collar up.

Chapter 6
Surprise

EARL FENNIMORE mumbled his way through the meadow toward his still in the twilight before dawn. He carried a rifle. From the edge of the trees, he wove his way inside.

Quill Rose rose up from among the whiskey barrels. He leveled his revolver at Fennimore. "Time's come to see the judge, Earl," he said, his voice flat, emotionless.

Fennimore, startled, brought his rifle up but stopped when he heard the click of a hammer being drawn back. He peered through the gloom. "That you, Quill Rose?"

"'Tis."

"Figured you'd come for me some time, but at the farm, not up here."

"What kind of rifle have you got there, Earl?"

"A Mauser."

"Lay it on the ground. That way I won't have to shoot you."

Earl Fennimore, a thick set, big-bellied man, leaned down. He placed his rifle by his feet and straightened up, still peering into the gloom.

"Step away from it, Earl."

Fennimore took one step back, jolting himself as

he backed into the trunk of a hackberry tree.

"Where's Bobby Ray?" Rose asked.

"Behind you. We never come into camp together. Bobby Ray, you there?"

Rose felt a ring of steel press into his back. He spun around, flinging out his gun hand, his revolver catching the man behind him under the ear and knocking him off his feet.

The man clutched at the side of his head. "Run, Earl, run!" he hollered.

Rose fell on the man's chest. He pinned him to the ground and shoved the barrel of his revolver into the man's face. "Knew you had to be around here someplace, Bobby Ray. Now I'll tell you what, you stay right here or you'll wish to God you had."

Rose jumped up. He raced through the ash and the dogwoods after Fennimore. At the edge of the grove, he saw Fennimore ahead of him, running hard through the tall grass some eighty yards distant he estimated.

Rose stopped. He braced his arm against the trunk of a mountain ash and leveled his revolver over his arm. Rose sighted along the barrel, held his breath, and squeezed the trigger.

Fennimore fell forward.

Rose holstered his weapon and walked back into the grove, to Bobby Ray Reilly whimpering where he had fallen among the barrels.

Reilly pawed at the side of his head, his hand showing blood. "Did ya kill him? Did ya kill Earl?"

"I brought him down. He's out there in the meadow. Get to your feet, Bobby Ray, you've got work to do." Rose gathered up the two loose rifles and took a seat on a stump. "Bobby Ray, you pile the empty barrels, the copper coil, everything on the still's woodpile and set it afire."

"All of it?"

"Every last stick. When you've got a good fire going, I want you to take that axe over there and bust up your mash barrels."

"The beer'll ruin on the ground."

"You got that right, Bobby Ray. You're out of the business, so do it."

"Come on, Quill, have a heart."

Rose raised Reilly's rifle. He squeezed off a round, blowing two staves out of a mash barrel, releasing the juice that had been ready to run through the coil. "I've got the job started for you, Bobby Ray. Time to finish it."

WHEN THE FLAMES reached tree-top level, Rose and Reilly moved out of the grove, Reilly ahead of Rose, Rose carrying the arsenal.

Moaning came from the meadow.

Reilly broke into a run. "You alive, Earl? I'm a-comin', Earl!"

Rose charged after him, leaping, trying to see ahead, glancing this way and that for the other shiner.

Reilly got to him first, found Fennimore laying in the grass, clutching his leg and rocking.

"Damn sheriff shot me, Bobby Ray. Why the hell didn't you kill him when you had the chance? I'd a kilt him for you."

Reilly knelt down. "He was too fast, Earl. See? He

got me right under the ear."

Fennimore swatted Reilly in the other ear, sending his hat flying. "Hell, Bobby Ray, he shot me in the leg!"

Rose leveled a rifle at the quarrelers. "Now, boys, I hate to interrupt this family reunion, but I've gotta see something."

He shoved Reilly out of the way and grabbed Fennimore's boot. He pulled it up to get a better look at the heel.

Fennimore howled.

"Earl, you're not gonna die, so shut up."

Rose pulled hard on the boot, and Fennimore howled again. Rose ran a hand over the heel and found what he was looking for.

"This is gonna convict you, Earl. Attempted murder twice, murder once." He let go of the boot. It and the wounded leg fell to the ground. "Earl, I've gotta know, why'd you shoot that man down from your still?"

"He was pokin' around where he had no business."

"Did you know him?"

"Hell no."

"Least you could have buried him."

"Aww, we left him there for the bears to drag off."

"Earl, get up. Let's go see the judge. You've been wanting a ride to the state prison, and now you're gonna get one."

THE TRIAL lasted all of five minutes. K.W. Lingenfelter, the county attorney, called only one witness—Quill Rose.

"Show him," he said to Rose after Rose took his place in the witness chair.

Rose dug two shells from his pocket. He handed the shells to Judge Enos Limke. "Luther Click found these among the boulders up by Earl and Bobby Ray's still."

Next, he passed two Mauser rifles over. "I confiscated these from Earl and Bobby Ray. The firing pin markings on the shells could have been made by either gun."

As a final exhibit, he handed up Fennimore's boot. "Belongs to Earl. I took it from him. If you'll look at the heel, you'll see a corner of it busted away. The print made by that boot matches the prints in the dirt coming down out of those boulders where the shooting took place."

Limke touched the heel. "Anything else?"

Rose leaned back in the witness chair. "Just this. The man murdered up in the mountains, I buried him. Earl admitted to me that he shot him, that he left the body for the bears to drag away."

Limke aimed the hammer end of his gavel at Fennimore. "Is that true?"

Fennimore, silent, stared at the boot on the judge's desk.

"Bobby Ray?" Limke asked, pointing his gavel at Reilly.

"Yessir?"

"Is that true?"

Fennimore slapped Reilly's shoulder.

Reilly, grimacing, grabbed at his upper arm. "Earl, I ain't takin' the blame for ya. Judge, I didn't kill that man, an' I didn't shoot that other one, neither."

"The federal man?"

"We done heard he was comin' fer us, so we waited on him. Earl put two holes in him. We was sure he was dead, so we got the hell outta there."

Limke massaged his forehead. He drew his hand down his face after which he turned to the jury. "What say you, guilty?"

The foreman glanced to those on either side of him and got nods in return.

"Well?" Limke asked.

The foreman nodded, too. "Yessir, guilty on all charges."

Limke rapped his gavel on the wood block on his desk. "This court's record shall show a verdict of guilty. Bobby Ray? Earl? Stand up."

After much shuffling, both men, shackled, got to their feet behind the defense table, Fennimore ramrod straight, Reilly leaning forward on his knuckles on the table.

"Bobby Ray, I hereby sentence you to twenty years in Brushyfork State Prison. Earl? You're going to forfeit your life for this one. Death by electrocution."

Chapter 7
A final act

LATE SUMMER gave way to early fall, and Eamon McCool sat in the sun on Luther's front porch, Schroeder examining his repairs to McCool's arm.

"No need to keep you around any longer," Schroeder said after he packed his tools back in his bag. "You, my friend, are pretty well healed up. You can take care of yourself. You don't have to lean on Luther to get around like you used to."

"Doc, I appreciate all you've done for me."

"It's Luther here. If he hadn't found you—"

Luther blushed, the color deepening his tan.

McCool grabbed Luther's hand. "My horse—"

"Found her where you said she'd be, still hobbled in that mountain meadow, gettin' fat on the sweet grass and keepin' tanked up at the stream." He went to the springhouse and returned with a pair of saddlebags, weathered some from being in the outdoors for the weeks since McCool had left his horse for the foot climb into the high mountains. "Your badge an' your revolver are in here. Why didn't you take 'em with you?"

"Luther, I figured if anyone got the drop on me, I could talk my way out. A gun and I'd be in trouble. A badge and I'd be dead."

"You come close to bein' dead."

"Close counts only in horseshoes. Luther, I've bagged me twenty-seven moonshiners, and not one ever got a shot off at me. I just didn't think these fellers were out there. I was told they were on the other side of the mountain. I was careless. I wasn't watching."

Schroeder settled on his haunches. He looked up at McCool. "If you're thinking of going back into law work, I'd advise against it."

McCool rubbed his right arm, at the twinge of pain that was still there. "Why?"

"It's that arm. It's never going to be strong. The ulna was shot up. Any sharp movement could break it again. Even firing your revolver, the recoil—"

"Then I'll have to learn to shoot left-handed."

EVERY DAY for the next two weeks, McCool hiked up on Gobbler's Knob, not far from where he had been shot. There he practicing drawing with his left hand and firing at stones with his left hand. He burned through forty-three boxes of cartridges, honing his speed and accuracy.

On the last day, Quill Rose and Luther hiked up with McCool, Rose handing him a right shoulder holster of the kind a left-handed shooter requires. When they got to the boulder patch, Rose waved McCool on. After he had passed from sight, Rose, with Luther's help, set up three targets ten yards to the side and down from the boulders.

"Time to show how good you are," Rose called out.

"I'm ready," McCool's voice came back.

Rose and Luther moved away, Rose calling out, "On three . . . One, two, three!"

McCool came bursting around the boulders, running hard. He drew and threw two shots at the first target and two more at each of the remaining targets without slowing his run. With his gun empty, McCool let up. He stopped and leaned down, breathing hard, his hands on his knees. "How'd I do?"

Rose and Luther examined the targets, Rose shaking his head. "Can you believe this?"

Luther touched one of the bull's eyes. "Not if I hadn't seen it."

"Well, how'd I do?"

Rose swivelled to McCool. "Six shots. Two to the center of each."

"How about that." He straightened up and shook the empty cartridges out of his revolver's cylinder. "Nobody will ever get me if it comes to a gunfight."

"Do better. Don't get yourself in a position where you have to be in a gunfight."

LUTHER SHUFFLED into his kitchen the next morning, scratching at his ribs. He lit a fire in the cookstove and started the coffee. Something, though, distracted him— a note on the table. He moseyed over, a can of ground beans in his hand, and read down the paper: **Friend, left before sun-up to catch the lumber express at Townsend. Come by the depot and the stationmaster will have something for you from me.**

LUTHER AMBLED into the railyard, a bulging tow sack over his shoulder. He spied a conductor hurrying toward the caboose of a train being made up. Luther waved to him, calling his name.

The conductor waved back. He detoured to Luther. "You got the usual?" he asked.

Luther passed him the tow sack. "Three gallons of my best shine. You'll get it to the judge at the courthouse?"

"Always do. I'll have your money for you tomorrow, minus my delivery fee. If you can't get in, I'll leave it with the Crock."

The Crock—Crockett Walker, the stationmaster— Luther's next stop. He bobbed his head to the conductor and went on to the depot, picking his way through piles of freight that had come off the Number Three from Maryville. Luther tapped on the counter.

Walker, at his desk, spun around in his chair. He threw up his hands. "Luther!"

Luther leaned against the counter. "I unnerstand you got somethin' for me."

"That I do." The stationmaster, a heavyweight, took a paper from the top of his out-box and horsed himself up from his chair. He played with the paper, keeping the front toward himself as he came over to the counter. "That fella you looked after—"

"Mister McCool?" Luther asked.

"That's him. He sent a telegram to his boss at the district Treasury office in Johnson City this morning, saying he's quit to find himself a safe job—as a bank guard."

"Really? He did that?"

"Yup, then he scratched out this note to you." Walker laid the paper on the counter. He turned the paper to Luther. "He couldn't say enough good things about you."

Luther placed a hand on either side of the note and read. He jacked up an eyebrow. "Don't know what to make of this."

Walker twisted the paper back to himself. He folded it and tucked it into the top pocket of Luther's bib overalls. "It's simple. You saved the life of this fella. You took care of him while he was on the mend. This is his way of thanking you. He's give you his horse, saddle and all, a fine animal, I saw it. It's waiting for you at the livery stable."

The Box Social

*Note: Today, a lot of elementary schools hold carnivals to raise money for classroom supplies. Back seventy-five years ago and more ago, when most elementary schools were one-room country schools, the box social was the fundraiser. And they were social events. Everybody came.

LUTHER CLICK, a banty rooster of a man, though on the quiet side, arrived at the Skuppernong School that fall Friday evening before anyone else. He tied his sorrel mare to the rail fence at the side of the building and strolled over to peer in the window.

Nothing, he noticed, absolutely nothing changed in the little school since he had worked his way through all the readers when he was a child some forty years before—the teacher's desk on the platform, the blackboard on the wall behind, above the blackboard the letters of the alphabet in cursive— black, painted on the white wall by a Mister Wilcox, one of the school's first teachers, a man who had what Luther's mother had called beautiful handwriting.

A picture of George Washington hung to one side

of the alphabet, to the other side, a picture of Abraham Lincoln, and right in the center—above the alphabet— on a stick poking into the room from the wall, the flag of the United States of America, a bit faded now.

Luther peered around for the bench where he had sat when he was a student, disappointment showing in his face when he realized it was not there.

There had been a change. Desks now occupied the center of the room. He counted them—twenty-four. How could that be enough? Most years, when he was a student, thirty children attended Skuppernong, and one year, there were thirty-six. Of course, of the thirty-six, seven were Clicks. There also were six Belsons and five Tibbetses. Three families accounted for half the students that year.

He climbed the steps to the front door and just naturally put his hand on the doorknob. And he did as he had done when he was a child, he turned it.

The door opened.

The school had never been locked when Luther was a student that he could remember, and it still was not locked.

He took a cautious step inside, and the familiar odors of chalk dust and old books swept over him. He even thought he smelled the lilac water Miss Campbell had worn every day during the two years Luther had worked his way through the third, fourth and fifth readers.

There was the big wood-burning stove where children put their mittens to dry after recess in the winter, the stove that could roast your backside in less than a minute when the damper was open, when the flames roared up the chimney like so many bellowing lions.

Luther's gaze drifted to the side wall, and there it was—his bench. He saw the initials he had carved into the edge of the board seat.

Oh, what a boy can do with a Buck knife.

Mister Dobbs had thrashed him for that.

All the benches were there, pushed up against the side walls. Luther wandered over. He ran his fingers across the initials. His fingers hadn't forgotten the feel of the letters even though the sharp edges had been worn smooth over the years.

He sat down.

Luther closed his eyes, and he was a child again. And there in his memory he saw her, Miss Kronvick, leading the fifth reader students in reciting the times tables.

. . . four times three is twelve, four times four is sixteen, four times five is twenty . . .

And there was his brother Bill standing by her desk, reciting 'The Rhyme of the Ancient Mariner.'

"Excuse me."

Luther's eyes flicked open, and he found himself staring up at a beefy young woman.

How long had she been there?

"I'm Miss Brown. I'm the teacher here."

Luther scrambled to his feet. He snatched his hat from his head and held it in front of him, that awkward way a child would. "I'm Luther Click, ma'am. I used to sit right here when I was a kid." He motioned at the bench. "See the initials? They're mine."

"You certainly left a mark on the school, Mister

Click. I surely hope the school left a mark on you."

Miss Brown laughed.

There was that hint of lilac water, Luther was sure of it.

"Click?" the teacher asked, mulling over the name. "I don't have any Click children in my classes."

"No, ma'am. My brothers and sisters, those still alive, moved away. I'm the only one that lives near the school. I never married."

"If you don't have children here, how did you find out about our program?"

"Neighbors invited me. They got children, the Andersons and Missus Tatum."

"Oh, the Tatum twins, Amanda Jane and Willy. They are bright ones, aren't they? That Amanda Jane just is devouring the first reader."

Luther shifted his weight. "Well, I 'spect you'd like me to get out of here so you can get things set up."

"Oh, no, you're fine just where you are, Mister Click. Just one thing." Miss Brown gestured toward a box that rested on the corner of her desk, a white box that had a large red-ribbon bow on it. "That's mine, for the social. I'd appreciate it if you didn't bid on it. I've got a young man, you see."

"Who that be?"

"Horace Tanner. Do you know him?"

"The Tanners, yeah. Your fella, he works the farm with his pa, doesn't he?"

"That's Horace."

"You picked a good 'un, Miss Brown. You surely did." Luther backed toward the door.

"You'll help me, won't you?"

"I surely will, ma'am."

Luther heard horses trotting up the road toward the school, pulling a farm wagon that clattered when it bounced over bumps and banged through ruts.

Soon some twenty families were there, arriving by means of shays, buckboards, and wagons. None drove cars, although a few farmers in the cove had Model T's they'd adapted for farm work. The rears of the cars were usually on blocks and a tire belted to a pump, saw or grist mill. One farmer used his T to pull a plow.

The families packed the school, filling even the folding chairs brought in from the Grange hall. Several late arrivals stood outside the open windows.

Miss Brown stepped forward, waving for order. "It's time we got started," she said. "I've asked Luke Tanner to lead us in the Pledge of Allegiance."

Tanner, barefoot and in bib overalls like most of the other boys, came up on the platform. He put his hand over his heart.

Everyone shuffled to their feet and, when the room became quiet, Tanner started: "I pledge allegiance—"

Everyone recited the words with him. When Tanner reached the end, he marched back to his desk.

Miss Brown came to the front of her desk. "I want to welcome everyone here to the Skuppernong School," she said. "Before we auction off the box suppers, the children wish to present a brief program."

She stepped aside, and the students came forward in groups of twos and threes—some alone—and sang a song or recited a poem or a story.

The Tatum children sang 'Bluejean Jim and Gingham Sue.' Janey Leigh, their mother—a widow—

had made a gingham sunbonnet for her daughter, and her son wore his grandfather's straw hat that was a good three sizes too large. It slipped over his eyes while he sang, and he forever pushed it up with the heels of his hands.

All applauded, but the greatest applause came for the Grunstad boy when he finished his recitation of Henry Wadsworth Longfellow's epic poem, 'The Midnight Ride of Paul Revere.'

Miss Brown knew how to build a program, Luther thought. Little Adolphus was a showstopper.

She thanked the children and then called on school trustee Elroy Masters to cry the auction.

"No IOUs, gentlemen," Masters called out as he waved his hands for everyone to become quiet. "This is strictly a cash-money transaction. We need to buy new arithmetic books and a big dictionary, and your dimes and dollars will help us, so bid high, everybody. I don't want nothing going for cheap here."

Luther saw several fathers slip coins to their ten- and twelve-year-old sons so they could bid.

"Now here's the rules," Masters said. "When you win the bid, you come up here and give your money to Miss Brown, and you take the box you bought. Now don't open it and don't start eating. When we sell the last box, the person who made your box will join you for supper. Sound good?"

Several men whooped and others clapped their well-callused hands together.

Masters picked up the box closest to him. He held it up for all to see—a fancy box decorated like a package one might find under a Christmas tree.

"Who will open for a quarter-quarter-quarter-quarter? Who will open for a quarter?" Masters chanted. "Who will open for a quarter-quarter-quarter-quarter?"

"Ten cents," Mister Tanner said from his place on a bench at the side of the room. He raised a hand, acknowledging his bid.

His wife jabbed him, the glare in her eyes announcing that that was not her box supper.

"Got a dime, who will go fifteen? Somebody gimme fifteen, fifteen, fifteen, gimme fifteen."

Someone outside a window waved.

"Twenty," said a man inside.

"Twenty-five," said the man outside.

Masters seesawed the bidding from there by pennies to thirty-four cents.

"Sold for thirty-four to somebody outside," Masters called out and picked up the second box. "Oh, this one is heavy. Lotta food in here. Come on, you big eaters, somebody open for a dime."

The dime came, and Masters rocked the bidding back and forth until he got eighteen cents.

"All right, now the third box—" Masters held up a new box. "—isn't it a beauty with this little shock of wheat tied to the top?"

He lifted the top and sniffed the contents. "Fried chicken and it does smell good. Come on, Ed Williams, open for twenty cents. I know you've got it and a lot more because I saw you sell a hog yesterday."

Williams nodded.

Another man chimed in twenty-five, Williams twenty-six, the other twenty-seven, Williams twenty-eight.

Masters cajoled for another penny. "Twenty-nine?" he asked. "Twenty-nine? All right, going then for twenty-eight cents to Ed Williams. Going once? Twice? All done? All in? It's yours, Ed. Enjoy the fried chicken."

Masters sold three small boxes that appeared to have been prepared by girls to boys in the audience. The next box, also small, had orange construction-paper pumpkins on it.

"Who will give me a nickel for this fine box supper?" Masters called out as he held the box high.

Willy Tatum jumped to his feet. "I got a penny!"

Masters smiled at the boy. "Have you got more?"

"Just a penny."

Masters gazed over the audience. "What do you think, should we let this young fella have this fine box supper for a penny?"

Applause came.

Masters went down to where Willy Tatum stood and handed him the box. "Young man, you just bought yerself a mighty fine supper."

Tatum pulled his penny from his overalls pocket. He gave the coin to the auctioneer who passed it onto Miss Brown.

Next Masters picked up the white box with the red ribbon. Miss Brown winked at Horace Tanner.

Tanner waved a hand at the auctioneer. "Fifty cents."

"Now that's more like it." Masters held the box high. "Who will gimme seventy-five?"

Luther, sitting next to Horace Tanner, touched the

brim of his hat.

Masters nodded. "I've got seventy-five, who will gimme a dollar?"

"Eighty," Tanner said.

"All right, I'll take eighty cents. Now let me have eighty-five, eighty-five, eighty-five, eighty-five cents." Masters looked around the room as he chanted. Luther thumbed the lapel of his coat.

"Eighty-five, who will go ninety? Ninety, ninety, ninety cents, who will go ninety?"

"Here," Tanner called out.

"Now ninety-five. Will somebody gimme ninety-five, ninety-five, ninety-five, ninety-five?"

Luther winked.

"Now a dollar. Who will go a dollar? A dollar, a dollar, a dollar, who will go one dollar?" Masters stepped forward. He spoke directly to the young Tanner. "Horace, you gonna let this get away from you? I get the feeling this is special."

"A dollar," Tanner said. He bobbed his foot.

"And a nickel? Who will give me a nickel more, a nickel, nickel, nickel more?"

Luther touched the corner of his eyebrow.

"Now I want a dollar and a dime, a dollar and a dime." Masters stared at Tanner. "You gonna let this fine box supper go because you're too cheap to go another dime? I know you want it."

"Who's got the bid?" Tanner asked, his foot bobbing at a furious speed.

"Don't worry about who has the bid. If the man wanted you to know, he'd announce himself."

"Pigs knuckles."

"What?"

"Pigs knuckles. I'm out."

"All right. Going once for a dollar and a nickel."

Luther slipped a quarter from the palm of his hand to between his thumb and forefinger. He tapped the back of Tanner's hand with the coin. "Don't let him get it away from you," he whispered.

Tanner took the quarter and shot to his feet, his grin as big as a summer sun. "A dollar twenty-five!"

"All right! Let's go for thirty. I got a dollar twenty-five, now I want thirty, thirty, thirty, thirty. Who will gimme thirty?"

Luther stared at the floor, and Masters stared at Tanner. "Thirty. Thirty, anybody? All right, it's going once for a dollar and a quarter. Going once? Going twice? All done? It appears your bid's good, young man. You've got it for a dollar and a quarter."

Tanner pounded Luther's back. "Mister Click, you're a savior!"

Luther gave a shy smile and shook his head.

Masters next held up a box wrapped in gingham cloth and tied with a yarn bow.

Pauline Tatum, the youngest of the four Tatum children, slipped away from her clan and came over to Luther. She stood at his knees. In her forever whisper she said, "That's my mommy's box."

Luther winked at the girl and lifted her to his lap.

"Well, this is a pretty one," Masters said of the box. "Surely I can get a quarter for an opening bid. Who'll gimme a quarter?"

Luther touched a finger to his nose.

"I've got the quarter. Who will go thirty, thirty,

thirty, thirty? Who will go thirty? Thirty? No one? All right, I'll take a penny for twenty-six."

It came from someone outside.

Masters ran the bidding by pennies up to thirty-one cents.

Luther tapped the back of his hand for thirty-two.

"All right, I've got thirty-two cents. Who will make it thirty-three? Thirty-three? Thirty-three? Thirty-three? The man outside, thirty-three? No? Then I'm letting it go for thirty-two. Thirty-two cents it is."

Luther gave a quarter, a nickel, and two pennies to Pauline Tatum and pointed her to the teacher. She ran out of the audience.

"Well, look at this? A girl bought this box supper." Masters stepped down to the floor and gave the box to Pauline. She took it and ran to her mother.

"Who gave you the money for this?" Janey Leigh Tatum asked, but the girl said nothing, merely worked her way onto the bench beside her mother and snuggled close.

After the last box sold, Miss Brown stepped to the blackboard and wrote in thick chalk numbers $12.67.

"There you have it, folks," Masters said. "That's generosity, and we can buy books with that."

People applauded. Then they turned to the serious business, the women—and girls—identified themselves to the men—and boys—who had bought their box suppers. Next came the search for desks, chairs, platform space, and benches where the couples could eat together.

Several buyers found they got more than they had bargained for. Horace Tanner spread a blanket on the grass outside and lit a lantern so he and Miss Brown could see what they were about to eat when up rushed six of the teacher's smaller students intent on eating with her.

Luther got not only Janey Leigh Tatum, but her daughters, Pauline and Mary Sue.

Willy Tatum won the right to eat with an embarrassed eight-year-old beauty, Bethy Anne Tanner.

Amanda Jane Tatum—Willy's twin—had joined the gaggle of children with Miss Brown and Horace.

Elroy Masters' brother Enos, another small man like Luther and, like Luther, a bachelor, found himself diving into a box of ham and candied sweet potatoes with Ed Williams' spinster sister, Ethel, who tipped the scales at two hundred thirty pounds.

Masters, to his surprise, found that he had bought the supper box his mother had made.

Luther improvised an eating space with the saddle from his horse. He placed it on the floor, and Pauline and Mary Sue climbed aboard. For himself and Janey Leigh, he rolled out the canvas he had tied behind the saddle, and he invited the auctioneer and the auctioneer's mother to sit with them.

Over a supper of fried chicken, baked beans, and potato salad, Luther and Masters swapped stories about their days as Skuppernong students.

"I never put a black snake in Mister Egleston's desk like your brother Bill did," Masters said, waving a half-chewed chicken leg at Luther and laughing at the memory. "Mister Egleston was looking for his ruler, and I can still see his hair spring up on end when saw that thing looking at him, flicking out its tongue."

"Oh gawd, that was somethin', wasn't it?"

"Now Luther, you remember that old trapper who told us he had caught the most fearsome creature ever knowed to man up in the mountains," Masters went on, "and for a nickel a head he'd show us?"

Luther slapped his knee. "I can still see myself going out the window."

"Missus Tatum," Masters said after taking another bite from his chicken leg, "the man asked to use the school for a Saturday night, and he told everybody in the cove to come, and for a nickel each, he's show 'em this monstrous creature, a skyfloogle, he called it. He just packed the place and got the awfullest bag of coins in return. Remember, Luther, he had a canvas across the front of the platform?"

"Yup."

"That old trapper—" Masters dropped the leg bone in the box and wiped his fingers clean on his trouser legs. "—he got us all to hush up, and he went behind the canvas to make sure everything was ready, and we heard these chains a-rattling something fearsome and boards splintering and the most awful scream. That old man, his shirt tore and blood on him, he come running out from behind the canvas yelling: 'The skyfloogle's got loose! Run for your lives!'"

He shouted that directly at Pauline and Mary Sue, and, mouths gaping, they fell off the saddle.

Janey Leigh scooped them up before Luther could get to them.

Masters stopped. "Didn't mean to scare ye? Are you chillun' alright?" he asked.

Janey Leigh glanced at him as she settled her

youngest. "I think so."

Masters cranked back up. "Well, anyway, we saw something beating against the canvas, trying to get through it and it was just panic in here, wasn't it, Luther, grown men knocking people down to get out the door—" He fired a pointer finger at a window. "— you went out that window I think it was, right? And I went out the window down there, that old man diving out the same window after me. I tell you he hit the ground running."

Luther shook his head.

Masters did, too. "Oh, my, we all pulled foot for home. Luther, maybe you didn't know it, but the next day my pa and me, we come back to the school to get the horses we'd left behind. We expected to find them torn to pieces–dead–but there they were where we'd tied 'em to the fence down by the outhouse, dozing in the morning sun."

"Oh, no."

"Oh, yes. So we eased up to the window of the schoolhouse and stole a peek inside, and it was the awfullest mess—" Masters spread his arms wide. "—the benches upset, blood everywhere. But it was so quiet we figured that floogle thing had to be long gone back up into the mountains. So we went inside, and the canvas was still hanging there, tore but open."

Luther leaned forward. "What'd you find?"

"On the platform was chains and busted boards, but something didn't look right to Pap. No sir, he found a spot where the blood wasn't fully dry, and he knelt down there and he touched it. He worked some of it between his fingers—" Masters did the same rubbing motion with his fingers. "—finally, he put a dab on his tongue, and that's the only time in my life I ever heard him swear. "Damn," he said—excuse me, Mother—'It's catsup,' he said. We had been fooled royally."

Janey Leigh Tatum snapped her gaze from Masters to Luther and back to Masters. "Did you ever see that man again, the trapper?"

"No, ma'am, not one of us in the cove ever saw that old feller again, nor our nickels neither. Ever anybody tells you they been floogled, well, now you know where that comes from."

Janey Leigh gestured at the nearest window. "Mister Click, and that's the one you went out?"

Luther got up. He went to the window and ran his hand along the sill, thinking, remembering. "Yeah, this is the one, Missus Tatum." He came back, his hands thrust in his pockets. "It was one bodacious exit."

"Surely must have been."

"I came right down on the biggest bull thistle outside the window. Pa, he picked prickers out of me for a week."

The Fire Starters

*Note: A second novella, a story this time of misdirected revenge, community, and hard-won justice.

Chapter 1
The barking dog

OLD JIM, the Newfoundland, raised such a ruckus that Maybelle Anderson woke from a sound sleep. She rolled over to her husband and shook his shoulder.

"There's something outside, Rabun."

"Whaaaat?"

"There's something out there."

"Nooo."

"Jim's barking."

"Probably a skunk."

"Skunk or no, I can't sleep with all that noise."

"I can." Anderson pulled a pillow over his head.

"Rabun, get out there." She jabbed him in the back so hard he rolled out of bed and fell to the floor.

Anderson forced himself up on his hands and knees. He squinted across the bed at his wife. "Maybelle, this is cruel."

"Cruel or no, git."

He felt around for his shoes, found them, and sat on his rump to pull them on.

"If it's a skunk," Maybelle Anderson said, "get Old Jim in the kitchen before he gets sprayed."

Anderson stumbled out of the bedroom and down the backstairs. At the porch door, he turned back. Anderson gathered up his shotgun and, from a high shelf, took down two shells. These he dropped into the twin barrels and snapped the gun shut.

Outside, Anderson trotted toward Jim's barking, toward the barn, the cold air making him feel his age. He rounded the corner, and there stood the dog, yapping and clawing at the door.

Anderson grabbed the Newfoundland's collar. He shook him. "Hush!"

In the quiet that followed, Anderson heard something in the barn that, by its sound, didn't belong there.

He reached for the latch, and the door burst open, slamming into him, slamming him to the ground.

Something ran by, then another, their forms visible in the pale light of the sliver of moon that hung high in the night sky. Anderson whipped himself over onto his belly. He brought his shotgun around and jerked the trigger.

One blast and a scream. He'd put a load of bird shot into someone, he was sure of it. Then Anderson sensed it, light flickering behind him.

He swung around. "Oh God!"

Anderson scrambled to his feet. He ran inside where flames licked up a wall, ran to the far side of the barn and kicked open the door that led to the pasture. He chased his six milk cows outside, then hustled to the box stalls where Tom and Hank, two of his Percherons, whinnied and nickered—frantic. He opened their doors, caught each by the mane, and led them outside.

Mac and Bob, the other team of Percherons, screamed, terrified as flames swept across the ceiling above their stalls. Anderson ran back inside. He yanked open the door to Bob's stall, but the horse pulled back. He caught Bob's halter.

The horse reared and slashed a front hoof at Anderson.

Anderson grabbed a feed sack. He whipped it over the horse's eyes and pulled the sack tight to block out the light of the flames. In the melee, he yelled at the horse and pulled on his halter, and Bob came, the fire crackling around him.

Anderson turned the great horse loose. He slapped him on the rump, and the horse bolted out into the pasture.

The screams from Mac brought Anderson racing back to find flames eating away at the door to the horse's stall. He snatched at the latch and yanked back when the flames seared his fingers.

Anderson tried again to get the door open and again pulled back, the flames raging now, the heat so intense, the smoke chokingly thick.

Then he heard Mac fall.

Anderson gave it up. He staggered from the barn, fell to his knees, and wept.

HORACE TANNER saw the flames rising from the Andersons' barn from more than a mile away. He had been out with Ellie Brown, the school teacher, and had just left the home where she boarded. He turned his horse onto the road that led to the Andersons' farm and jammed his heels into the filly's flanks.

She leaped to a gallop and raced the mile to the Andersons' yard where she sped past a woman running from the house. Tanner didn't rein the filly to a stop until she came around to the pasture side of the barn. There he saw, silhouetted against the flames now raging up the outside wall, someone on his hands and knees.

Tanner leaped from his horse. He grabbed the man under one arm and dragged him away, the man reeking of smoke and the forearm of his long underwear burned away. "What happened, Mister Anderson?"

"Rabun! Rabun!" Maybelle Anderson called out, running up. She got her shoulder under her husband's other arm.

"Mac's dead—"

"No! Nooooo—"

A team and farm wagon clattered into the yard. "Whoa there! Whoa!" the driver shouted.

Warren Sweet slapped the reins into his wife's hands and jumped from the box. He trotted off to the Andersons and Tanner. "Saw the flames from our place! What the hell happened?"

Maybelle Anderson wiped at the tears in her eyes

with the sleeve of her nightgown. "He doesn't know, Warren."

Sweet looked hard at Anderson. "You get everything out?"

Anderson shook his head.

"Mac," Missus Anderson said. "Rabun said we lost him."

"Oh gawddamn. But you got the cows out, and the other horses?"

"I think he did."

"Praise the Lord. Rabun, let's get you over to the house. There's no savin' that barn. It's all a-fire now."

Nancy Ann Sweet hurried over after having driven her husband's team and wagon to the far side of the house, away from the blaze. She got her arm around her neighbor. "Come on, now. Come with me, Maybelle."

A little Chevy bounced through the yard toward the assembly and slewed to a stop by the steps to the kitchen. Elroy Masters bailed out—he, like Anderson, in his underwear. "Jesus Christ, what happened?" he asked when he got near.

Tanner and Missus Anderson let the old farmer down on one of the steps, his arm shaking, fire blisters covering his hand. Missus Anderson sucked in her breath.

Nancy Ann Sweet shook her neighbor. "Maybelle, tears don't help nothing. Now stop that." She peered into the confusion in the woman's eyes. "We need butter for Rabun's hand. Where do you keep your butter?"

Elroy Masters motioned at the hand. "I'd use axle

grease, Missus Sweet."

Horace Tanner stepped in. "My gramma, she swears by the scrapings of the inside of a white potato to draw the fire out. Then you put on a salve of talcum powder and Vaseline."

Nancy Ann Sweet looked away from the men. "In the spring house?" she asked the elderly woman.

Missus Anderson nodded.

She took hold of her husband. "Warren, we got to have that butter."

He turned and sprinted for the spring house, calling out when he ran back, a crockery dish in his hands, "Got it!"

She grubbed up a ball of butter the size of a goose's egg and worked the hardness out of it. Then she slathered it over Anderson's scorched arm, hand, and fingers, he winching. "Warren, go in the house and find a towel. We got to wrap this."

Sweet moved around Anderson and bounded up the steps.

"I don't know," Masters said, "I've seen some granny women use salt water, others the powder of hot coals."

"Elroy, that's nonsense. What I'm doing is right."

Old Jim, the Newfoundland, pushed through the people crowded around Anderson. He sat on his haunches in front of the old man and put his head in Anderson's lap.

The old man caressed the massive head with his good hand. "You all right, boy?"

The dog whimpered as if he knew the depth of the disaster that had befallen the family.

A creaking sound came, like pegs being torn loose

from timbers. Those around Anderson turned and saw, with him, the barn walls lean in. A moment and the entire structure caved in on itself, billowing a plume of sparks above the flames, sparks that drifted away toward a hayfield rich with green meadow grass not yet ripe for the harvest.

Tanner shaded his eyes. "Thank God the breeze is blowing that way. It's carrying the cinders away from the buildings."

Masters kicked at a weed by the steps. "Do you know what caused the fire, Rabun? You didn't have no hot hay in there, didja?"

Anderson gazed up, dazed. "Someone burned us out."

"No."

"Two men. I shot one, running away."

"Know who?"

"No idee."

Masters pulled young Tanner aside. "Horace, I've got me a revolver in my car. Let's see what we can find."

The two hurried off.

Maybelle Anderson sat down beside her husband. She took his aged face in her hands. "It's gone, Rabun. Everything we worked a lifetime for—it's gone."

She buried her head in his shoulder and wept. He laid his good arm around her and felt the sobs racking her body.

Warren Sweet touched Anderson's shoulder. "Rabun, if you'd like, I'll take your horses to my barn. I've got some extra space."

"Would you do that?"

"Surely, neighbor. And I'll talk to John Oliver for you. Maybe he can take your cows. He and his boy milk a fair number already."

MASTERS AND TANNER stumbled around in the hayfield in the semi-dark that precedes dawn, Masters parting a bunch of grass with his shoe. "Tanner? Anything over your way?"

"Dead cat. That's all I've found."

"Well, I say we give it up. I'm thinking I'd better get me into Townsend and call the sheriff. A fire and shooting, this is his business now."

MASTERS STOOD by his car, beating on the side of Grumble Jones' house.

A bedroom window above went up and someone leaned out—Jones, bleary eyed. "Who is it? Who's out there?"

Masters stepped out where Jones could see him.

"Elroy?"

"Yeah!"

"What the hell you doin' out there in your underwear?"

"Been a fire out at the Andersons! Gotta use the telephone at your store to call the sheriff."

"Great Jesus." Jones slammed the window down so hard the glass cracked.

The sound came of bare feet slapping down the stairs. The door flew open, and Jones pounded out onto the porch and into the street, his nightshirt flapping behind him, he clutching a pair of britches in his hand.

Masters ran hard to catch up.

Both turned onto Main Street and didn't slow until they hit the boardwalk in front of Jones' store. The storekeeper fumbled in the britches' pocket for a key, came up with it, and jammed it into the lock.

"Gawddammit, Masters, my rooster ain't even up yet."

"Sorry, Grumble."

"How the hell did it happen?"

"Rabun says somebody put a match to his barn."

"Who the hell would do that? Everybody likes the family."

"Don't know."

Jones wrenched the door open. He lit a lantern and led Masters to his store's telephone.

Masters took down the receiver. He cranked the ringer and listened. When no one answered, he cranked the ringer a second time.

A voice, angry, came through the receiver Masters held pressed to his ear. "Whoever the hell you are, this better be gawddamn important. Elberta's sick."

"Benny?" Masters asked, speaking into the telephone's mouthpiece. "Benny Lawson, that you?"

"Yeah. Who is this?"

"Elroy Masters. From down in the cove."

"Elroy? Elroy, you don't got no phone."

"I'm at Grumble Jones' store. Would you ring up the sheriff for me? Call him at his home in Maryville."

Lawson swore and mumbled something about this not being his job while he rang through to the

Maryville operator.

Masters, waiting, watched Jones pull on his pants and tuck the tail of his nightshirt in, watched him go down the shelves, looking for a pair of shoes his size.

"Quill Rose here," said a new voice through the receiver.

Masters turned back to the wall phone. "Quill? Elroy Masters. Someone up here set fire to Rabun Anderson's barn. Two men, Rabun says. He may have shot one."

"Mister Anderson all right?"

"Burned some by the fire."

"Jesus. All right, I'll be up on the morning train."

A click and a hum came across the line, so Master's hung the receiver back on the wall phone's hook. He turned to Jones chewing on a soda cracker he'd taken from a barrel. "Quill says he'll be up on the Number Five."

"Aw, hell. Luther Click and his new family are coming home on that train. They're gonna have to see that same gawddamn mess." Jones held a fistful of crackers out to Masters. "Tell you what, Elroy, you go on home. I'll meet 'em and bring 'em all down to the cove. This is gonna be hard on 'em."

"Hard on everybody."

"'Tis. You go on now. I might as well do some work around the store as long as I'm here. Get things ready for my men."

Masters took some of the crackers and backed toward the door. "Well, thank you, Grumble."

"Yeah." Jones, pawing in his cash box, didn't look up. "You see my spare spectacles?"

Chapter 2
The return of Luther Click

JONES HAD FINISHED winding the stem of his railroad watch when he heard two short blasts and a long wail of a steam whistle coming over the trees from the west. He got up from the running board of his touring car, checked the time, and stuffed his watch back in his pocket.

Dammit to hell, she's on time.

Jones watched the Number Five slow as it came around the bend. Much closer, he saw two men burst from the station door, Bud Freedle, a freight handler, and the stationmaster, Crockett Walker, Walker with a mass of papers in his hand.

Two wagons from the cove, loaded with eight-gallon cans of milk, rolled up next to Jones' car while his attention was on Freedle and Walker. The jangling of the metal rings on the horses' harnesses caused the storekeeper to glance over at them.

Ed Williams called down to Jones from his perch on the buckboard. "Hear about the fire, Grumble?"

"Yeah. Damnedest thing. I've gotta tell Luther and Janey Leigh. They're on the train, just gettin' back from their weddin' trip."

"It's gonna break Janey's heart."

"Any idea who the sonsabitches are who set the

fire?"

"Lotta guessing, but nobody knows."

"Somebody will spill the beans. Quill Rose is on the train. He'll see to that."

The Five rolled to a stop with a boxcar next to Williams' wagon. Freedle, who had climbed into the car from the station side, rolled the door open.

Williams stepped over the board seat into the box of the wagon. "Grumble, if you'll excuse Ronnie and me, we've got to get our milk on the boxcar for the return run to Maryville."

"Sure, you do that."

Williams swung the first can across the gap to Freedle.

Jones turned away, toward the Pullman, toward a tall, lean man swinging down the steps, Luther Click behind him.

Jones waved.

Quill Rose—the lean man in his only suit, Navy wool—extended his hand to Jones. "Grumble, Simms told me Luther and his family were on the train, so I rode up with them, told them what little I know."

"Nobody hurt, was there?" Luther asked.

Jones rubbed at his face, then gazed at Luther for a long time.

"Well?"

"Elroy told me your father-in-law, Mister Anderson, he got pretty bad burned, trying to get the horses out of the barn. I've already sent Doc Schroeder out, but I wouldn't tell Janey Leigh just yet."

Worry lines trenched into Luther's face. "If you think that's best."

"Shh. Here she comes."

Simms, the conductor, helped Janey Leigh Click and her four children down the Pullman's steps, Crockett Walker behind them, carrying their suitcases and bags.

Jones waved Walker over. He opened the trunk of his car, and the two men stuffed the bags in while Quill Rose and Luther packed the family and themselves into the car.

"What do they know?" Walker asked Jones, keeping his voice low, as he shoved the last bag into the trunk.

"About as much as you."

"That ain't much, Grumble."

"No, it's not."

"Well, if there's any way I can help—"

"Do what you do best, Crockett. Listen for the gossip. Somebody's bound to spill." Jones squeezed Walker's shoulder, then closed the trunk and pushed himself in behind the steering wheel. He started the car and waved to Walker as he pulled away.

Silence slipped into what few open spaces existed around Jones, Rose, Luther, Janey Leigh, and the children.

Janey Leigh, in the backseat, hugged her two youngest daughters to her. Luther, also in the backseat, held Amanda Jane on his lap. They stared out the window at the fields and hills that passed by.

Quill Rose, sitting in the front, worked the brim of his hat around in his hands while Grumble Jones held tight to the steering wheel, looking as far up the road as he could. Willy Click, between them, glanced up first at one man and then the other. Neither spoke to him, so he went to studying his shoelaces.

"Mister Jones," Janey Leigh said.

Jones glanced up at the mirror, at the image of Janey Leigh Click leaning forward. "Yes?"

"Do you know anything the sheriff hasn't told us?"

"A little."

"What is it?"

The sun glinted off something ahead. Jones peered up the road at a car topping a rise, hurtling his way. "Here comes the man we should talk to."

He slowed his car and pulled it crosswise on the road.

The approaching vehicle also slowed, Doc Schroeder's Cadillac. It swayed up beside Jones' Kissel.

"Janey Leigh, Luther, think you should come with me," Jones said as he got out. "Quill, you look after the children?"

SCHROEDER, A SLIGHT paunch pushing against his belt, disgorged himself from his car. He reached a hand out to Janey Leigh as she, Luther, and Grumble Jones came over. "Janey Leigh, I don't know if Grumble told you, but your pa was burned in the fire."

"Oh no—" She turned to Luther, grabbed his hand, fear in her eyes.

"Now it's not all that bad, just a hand and his arm—his right arm." Schroeder stepped around to where he could talk to both Janey Leigh and Luther. "He got a good roasting, but I think he'll heal. He'll be able to work with his horses again and probably even be able to milk his cows. But he's going to be pretty shaky when you see him."

Luther rubbed his new wife's hand with a tender touch. "How long to heal, Doc?"

"I don't know. Three, four, five months maybe. There's not a lot we can do but wait. The body will take care of itself the best it can. You want me to tell the children?"

"Would you?" Janey Leigh asked.

"For you, yes."

Schroeder went over to Jones' car and poked his head in one of the windows. "Amanda Jane, Willy, girls, you remember me?"

"You're the doctor," Amanda Jane said.

"Would you like to come walk with me a bit? Sheriff, maybe you'd like to come along, carry the littlest one."

"Sure, Doc." Quill Rose opened his door. He got out and opened one of the back passenger doors for the girls. He picked up Mary Sue and held a hand out for Amanda Jane.

Schroeder gathered up Pauline and reached down for Willy's hand.

They walked off into a pasture, toward a small grove of choke cherry trees.

"Pauline, Amanda Jane, Mary Sue, Willy," Schroeder said as they moved along, "your grandpap's been hurt, and I want to tell you everything I can about it."

"Is he gonna be all right?" Pauline whispered.

"I think so."

They came on a large, broad rock that jutted up

from the sod. Schroeder stopped and set Pauline on the rock. Amanda Jane and Willy scrambled up beside her.

JONES, JANEY LEIGH, and Luther watched from the distance, watched Schroeder gesturing with his hand and arm and saw how closely the children listened. They saw them nod and smile, and they could tell that Willy and Amanda Jane particularly were asking questions, although they wondered what those questions might be.

"Gawd, that man's good with children," Jones said as he watched the three older ones swinging from Schroeder's arms as they returned. Mary Sue, they saw, ran alongside, doing her best with her short legs to keep up.

Quill Rose strolled some distance behind.

Schroeder shooed the mass of giggling youths into Jones' car before he came over to Janey Leigh. "You've got four good ones there. They're ready to help their grandpa any way they can."

She reached for his hand. "You're the best, Doc."

"No, not hardly. I'll be by every chance I get to see how Rabun's doing. But I'll be straight with you, you see any sign of infection, if that arm gets to stinking, you send Luther for me, and we'll get your pa to Knoxville where the pros can lend us a hand."

Schroeder smiled, a bit stiffly. He bobbed his head and went back to his car, fired up the Cadillac, bounced it through the borrow ditch and around Jones' car. When Schroeder had the Cadillac back on the road, he roared away.

Chapter 3
Barn raising

THE FIRE BURNED for three days as a consequence of all the hay and ear corn that had been stored in the loft. When out, neighbors gathered and raked the ashes. They spread them to cool and picked through for horse shoes, rings from harnesses and other metal. These they tossed on a scrap pile.

On a day the ashes were finally cold, the men of the cove drove in with their horses and wagons. Working under Luther Click's direction, they shoveled the wagons full of ashes and hauled load after load into the fields where they spread them so the remnants of the fire could fertilize the soil.

That day, Ben and Harold Wright also drove in. They found Rabun Anderson sitting on a bucket turned upside down under a Kentucky coffee tree, Anderson listening to John Oliver, a neighboring farmer. The Wrights waved to Anderson as they strolled up. Anderson, in response, struggled to stand.

Ben Wright motioned to him to stay seated. "Rabun, you'll be needing timbers to frame up a new barn."

Anderson shook his head. "I've got no money to rebuild."

"For some things you don't need money."

Oliver wedged into the conversation. "That's what I've been telling Rabun. My boy and I, we've got logs we're willing to drag over and split for shingles for a roof."

Ben gazed at Anderson. "He'll give you the roof, we'll give you the timbers. We've already got 'em cut out and stacked at our mill."

"But Ben—"

"No 'buts.' This is a done deal."

An International truck loaded high swayed into the farmyard, Grumble Jones at the steering wheel, his son Earl beside him, and his foreman John Godby in the shotgun seat.

"Rabun," Jones called out, "where do ya want us to unload this stuff?"

Anderson, with John Oliver's help, pulled himself up and came down to the truck. "What is all this?"

Jones looked back over his shoulder. "Window glass, kegs of nails and bolts, strap hinges for doors, bags of cement, a half-ton of mixed sand and gravel, and the big prize—track for the hay loft, a hayfork carriage, and a brand-dang-new hayfork itself."

Anderson peered up at the load. "Mister Jones, I've got no money for this."

Jones mopped his forehead with a bandana. "Friend, money's the one thing ya don't need. My suppliers owed me favors, and they've give ya this." He pushed the door open, the door squalling on its hinges, and slid down to the ground. "With the Wrights' timbers and John's shingles, about the only thing ya need now is barn boards for the sidin' and planks for the loft floor."

Jones slipped his arm around Anderson's shoulder. "As to that, friend, Little River Lumber is gonna provide all ya need. Soon as your neighbors get the framin' up, Mister King says he'll send out a couple truckloads."

"My neighbors?"

"Hell, man, haven't ya heard of a barn raisin'? This thing's all set to go." He swung over to the Wrights. "When do ya think ya can have those timbers in here?"

Ben took a paper from his pocket and checked something off. "Tomorrow. We cut 'em last year, so they're all cured out."

"What's yer longest?"

"Twenty feet."

Jones turned to Anderson. "Rabun, how long was your barn?"

"Forty feet, and twenty wide."

"Gawddamn, I think we're in business."

Jones set to sketching a building plan on a Big Chief pad Earl handed down from the truck. He counted up the number of timbers needed by length and wrote those numbers on another sheet of paper. This he ripped out of the pad and handed to Ben Wright. "Now I'll send Earl, John, and maybe another man out with my International in the mornin'. You'll need both my truck and yours for a couple trips with all that weight."

Jones, not waiting for a response, marched away to the site he thought best for the new barn, his squad and Anderson, John Oliver, and the Wrights trailing in his wake. "Now those corner timbers and side timbers," he said, "I'll leave Earl here, and he and Horace Tanner can dig the holes to set the timbers in. We'll cement them suckers in there and, by gawd, they're gonna keep."

He put an arm around Rabun Anderson's shoulders again. "Rabun, you get us old soldiers workin' on this, and we don't build a barn to fall down."

"I don't know what to say."

"You don't have to say a thing. We're gonna have us a bunch of fun."

OLIVER AND HIS SON, Bill Jack, arrived first the next morning. Anderson heard them whistling and shouting as their teams of Shire draft horses dragged white oak logs up the road and into the farmyard.

Father and son pulled the grab hooks from the logs, and Bill Jack went about marking the logs for cutting.

Oliver waved to Anderson coming away from the house. "Hey, there, neighbor!"

"Hey, there."

"Champ Frye and Speed Ferguson will be by directly to help Bill Jack. Rabun, you got one good hand. How about you drive Bill Jack's team back to our place, and we'll drag some more logs over?"

Anderson's smile lit the morning.

He and Oliver met a parade of farm wagons bearing neighbors, ladders, buckets, tools, block-and-tackles, heavy ropes—anything and everything people thought might be needed. Two heavy haulers mingled in the parade—the Wright brothers' Reo and Jones' International, both loaded down with twelve-by-twelve timbers. Ed Williams, in his Model T pickup, brought up the rear, in the back of his truck a portable saw.

"Gonna be some day, isn't it, Rabun?" Oliver called out.

Anderson shook his head.

When they got back, the neighbors had wrestled the corners posts into their holes and were bracing them so Earl Jones and Horace Tanner could fill the holes with the concrete they had mixed. Earl figured a wheelbarrow and a half for each hole.

Other neighbors slid the side timbers into their holes and pounded bracing stakes into the ground. Then they stood by to nail brace boards between the stakes and the timbers, to keep the timbers standing square.

Ben and Harold Wright moved from timber to timber, checking them with a level before they let the men nail the bracing in place.

Luther showed others where he wanted them to chop notches in the tops and undersides of the twenty-foot pieces so they could be laid across the tops of the side and corner timbers. When the men had each twenty-footer ready, they laid it across three farm wagons, backed the wagons between the side timbers, and lifted the long timbers into place.

Williams and Elroy Masters set up the portable saw. They pounded iron rods into the ground to keep the saw from moving, then jacked up the rear of Williams' truck to run a drive belt from one of the wheels to the pulley on the saw. Williams had built jigs so he could cut precise forty-five and ninety-degree angles. No hand-sawing, he said, when he could avoid it. High production with speed, precision, and as little muscle power as possible, those, Williams said, were words to live by.

He had barely finished touching up the teeth on the saw when Bill Jack, Ferguson, Frye, and Masters toted over the first log. They laid it on the saw's carriage.

Williams fired up the Ford's motor and engaged first gear. He advanced the hand throttle until he had the saw turning at a speed he liked.

Together, the men cut the log into two-foot lengths.

Bill Jack and Frye hauled the lengths away and set about splitting them into shingles while Ferguson recruited other men to help carry and cut logs.

Each length had to be split in half, then quarters. The heartwood had to be split out and then the quarters split into boards the shingle makers called bolts.

Working with a froe and a mallet, Bill Jack said he could split each bolt into as many as four shingles. By his estimate, he needed five thousand for the barn roof and said he could make a thousand a day if Frye did all the other jobs—splitting out the bolts, trimming the bark from the edges, and stacking the finished shingles.

At mid-day, John Oliver checked on the shingle makers. He decided they needed a second crew of shingle splitters, so Oliver pulled in Hillard Waldrop and Vinson Pitts, two old neighbors who worked well together. To his surprise, Pitts had come expecting to make shingles, and Waldrop had wedges, a go-devil, a froe, and a mallet in the back of his wagon.

Neighbors teamed with neighbors, cutting, notching, and pegging corner braces. They used inch-square pegs cut from Locust wood for more strength than nails could provide.

A parade of buckboards and surreys came up the road while the men were lifting the first of the end timbers into place, the rigs driven by wives and daughters—the food brigade. The women parked their conveyances in such a way that they could serve off the backs and tailgates.

When all was ready, Maybelle Anderson clanged the dinner bell. Janey Leigh, Nancy Ann Sweet, and Minnie Masters bustled past her, each carrying a mammoth pot of black coffee. They set the pots on the porch and waited.

The men came in twos and threes, then bunches, none making a run on the food, coming as if they knew they had to wait.

W.H. Oliver, preacher at the cove's Primitive Baptist church, white-haired and with a full beard that made him look every bit the patriarch he was, climbed the steps to the farmhouse porch. He pulled off his felt hat and turned to his neighbors, most of whom were his parishioners. "Let us remember Him," he said, "who has made all this possible."

Preacher Oliver raised his face to the heavens. "Great God, Creator of this wonderful world, You who can turn tragedies into blessings, we come before You, humbled by Your glory. Thank you, Lord, for this fine day and these, Your children, who have come together to raise up a barn for our good neighbor. And we thank You now for this abundant spread of good food that has come from the bounty of Your earth. Bless it to us that it may give us the strength to continue on with this job until it is done. In your Son's most holy name we do ask it, Amen."

A chorus of amens passed among the assemblage.

Wives and mothers handed plates and eating utensils to their husbands and sons. The bachelors, like Horace Tanner, got what they needed from Maybelle Anderson and Janey Leigh Click. The men then wandered from buckboard to surrey, heaping their plates with everything from wild game stew, fried chicken and pot likker dumplings to squash casserole, baked cornmeal pudding, and chocolate cake.

Minnie Masters leaned into Janey Leigh. "I wanted to bring a devil's food cake, but Preacher Oliver would have condemned it. I can hear him: 'Devil's food for Christians? Shame on you.'"

The Wright brothers and Luther Click ate together, poring over Grumble Jones' sketch.

Ben touched one part of the drawing. "See here, Luther, if we put one beam and its support posts in eight feet from the north wall and the other beam and posts in eight feet from the south wall, you and Rabun can build box stalls for his horses on one side of the barn and a feed room and stanchioned stalls for the cows on the other side."

Luther massaged the stubble on his cheeks. "I can see that. Yessir, that'd give us a wide alley in the center of the barn. That'd be good." He moved his hand along the sketch. "How about we put doors at each end of the alley?"

Harold tapped his fork on the sketch. "Minute we

get those beams and posts up, we ought to lay the joists across. See here? Then crews can put in the corner bracing and the bracing between the joists and the side timbers."

Louise Oliver came by with her stack cake and set wedges on the Wrights' plates and Luther's.

Luther touched a finger to his eyebrow, his way of saying thanks.

IN MID-AFTERNOON, a hard rubber-tired Kissel truck rolled in from Little River's sawmill, stacked with planks for the loft floor. After the driver had backed the truck up to the barn, Luther Click and Elroy Masters passed the planks up to crews to nail down for the loft floor.

A dozen men laid the planks across the joists. Beginning at the north wall, they nailed the first set in, then positioned the next planks. An hour and they had the floor finished. At Rabun Anderson's insistence, they framed up an opening in the floor at the west end of the barn so a stairway could be brought up from below. Other farmers notched stringers and cut treads and risers, and hammered the pieces together. They positioned the finished stairway in the opening. Satisfied with the fit, they pegged the stairway to the joists and side timbers to keep it secure.

Elsewhere, another dozen men set the side timbers up for the second story of the barn. They cut and pegged in bracing, and notched and set in place the capping timbers to support the roof.

The Olivers, the Wrights, Rabun Anderson, and

Luther Click stood back to admire the work that had been done.

John Oliver clapped Anderson on the shoulder. "Rabun, I say we quit and pick it up here in the morning. Two more days and it's gonna be done."

He put two fingers in his mouth and let loose with a piercing whistle that caused even the farmers at the far end of the barn to look up. Oliver waved at them to come over. "Boys, it's quittin' time, boys. I know you've got chores waiting for you, and it's time to get to them. Tomorrow, we break into two crews. One will build the framing for the roof; the other, the box stalls, stanchions and feed room. Once we get the rafters up, everybody's going up and nail shingles. We want that roof done tomorrow. Sound good to you?"

Elroy Masters gazed around over the others, waving for them to call their agreement.

The calls came, then most gathered up their tools, hitched their teams to their wagons, and rolled on out. The train of wagons split at the Cades Cove Road. There the bulk of the drivers turned south, but a third turned north.

Oliver came over to the Wrights. "Boys, I'm gonna leave you the tough job. You figure out how we're gonna build those roof supports and how we're gonna get 'em up there. I don't want a dozen men squabbling over that tomorrow because they see six different ways to do it. You decide with Rabun. You make the plan. You give the orders. All right?"

Ben gazed at Rabun Anderson.

"What you decide," Anderson said, "that's the way we'll do it."

Oliver took off his hat. He slicked his hair back. "All right. Bill Jack, let's get on home. We still got us two sets of cows to milk."

After the Olivers left, Maybelle called the remaining men in for supper.

"Luther, you're staying here tonight," she said after she got everyone seated around her kitchen table.

"But I got chores to do."

"Janey Leigh and the children have gone back to your place. They'll take care of the chores and milk the cow. Ben, Harold, you might as well stay the night, too. No point in you driving home and having to turn around and drive back out when the sun comes up."

"What do you think, brother?" Ben asked.

"All right by me if it's no imposition."

"You boys can use my razor in the morning," Anderson said.

After supper, and after the Andersons had cleared the table of dishes, the men sat around and sketched at ideas for the roof. The original roof had been light in construction and had used a ridge pole. Because this time the rafters would be twelve-by-twelve timbers on four-foot centers rather that two-by-six planks, Ben suggested the timbers be morticed and pegged together at the peak, then windbeams be mortised and pegged into the rafters four feet below the peak.

Ben glanced up at his host. "You'll get a lot of strength this way. Plus it'll be a lot easier to hang the track for your hayfork from the windbeams than if you get us crowded up there under a ridgepole with no room to work."

He sketched a plan and did the math to determine

how long the rafter timbers had to be and where they had to be notched to fit down on the roof supporting timbers.

He and Harold agreed to make the first set in the morning, before the neighbors arrived, a set that would serve as the pattern for the additional ten sets that had to be built.

"We usually use one-inch boards for the roof lathing," Anderson said. "That's always been flimsy."

Harold looked over the sketches. "What say we use planks?"

"If we did that," Ben said, "Rabun, you'd want that roof to overhang on both ends of the barn." He scribbled some numbers on his pad. "By my calculation, we'd need thirty-six planks, each twenty-one feet long. We could send Elroy in with our Reo to get them."

Harold sat back in a chair. He gazed at his brother. "If we build those rafter-and-windbeam units on the ground, how do we get 'em up sixteen feet to the top of the loft walls? They won't fly themselves up there."

"We'll just have to horse 'em up—pull 'em up on ropes."

"Sixteen feet? How about this? How about we build them on the loft floor? Then we only have to get them up eight feet. We might even be able to build us a jig to lift them with."

GRUMBLE JONES, out the next day to see how the barn was progressing, looked over the contraption Harold Wright had created to hoist the rafter-and-windbeam units into place. He clapped Harold on the shoulder. "That has got to be the damnedest piece of jerry-rigging I've ever seen. But, damn, fella, it looks like it's gonna work."

By mid-afternoon, the men had the plank laths nailed across the rafter timbers.

Eighteen men perched on the east end of the laths—nine on each side of the roof—waiting for others to toss wood shingles up to them.

Luther organized the children to carry shingles up to the loft. Men on ladders then passed the shingles up to the nailers. The hammering became intense when all the roofers nailed away.

To make sure the roofers had enough shingles, John Oliver put a third set of splitters to work.

By the end of the day, the three crews had made the full five thousand.

By the end of the day, the roof was done.

On the third day, neighbors framed in the windows and doors for the lower level and built and hung a massive loft door on the west end the barn, a door that, when opened out, would permit Anderson to bring hay up and inside. John Oliver supervised the crew hanging the track beneath the windbeams. They also hooked in the hayfork carriage and ropes and pulleys to make the hayfork work.

Ben and Harold Wright directed the crew nailing on the barn board siding.

Luther Click worked with a third crew, nailing two-by-four soffits to the ends of the roof lathing. They also cut boards to plug the gaps between the rafters, the roof and roof supporting timbers, and nailed them in place.

A cheer went up when Rabun Anderson, at Oliver's insistence, hammered left-handed the last nail in.

Grumble Jones waved for everyone's attention. "Boys, you did a helluva job. But no new barn is complete until we have a barn dance. Tomorrow night, eight o'clock. Be here!"

Chapter 4
The tip

JONES WALKED Anderson around the finished structure. "Rabun, you got a damn good barn here. Can't wait to see it full of livestock. That's what barns are meant for."

Anderson teared up.

"Oh, come on now, I know you lost Mac. But you still got three horses, and you got all your cows."

A horn interrupted.

A Model T touring car bumped its way into the farmyard and stopped. A stranger climbed out, a stranger to all except Luther Click resting on a sawhorse.

"Who's that?" Anderson asked.

Luther came up. "Uncle Harley Reid from out Chestnut Flats way."

Jones stared at the new arrival. "By gawd, that is Harley. I see him maybe once a year at my store. Rough old coot. What he's doing here?"

The man, tall and gaunt, came around to the passenger door. He opened it and shagged out a youth. He pushed the boy along.

"Evening, Luther, Mister Jones," Reid said when he got closer. He looked to Rabun Anderson. "You be Mister Anderson?"

"Yessir."

"I be Harley Reid. Maybe you heerd about me? Luther has."

"Well, Luther knows just about everybody in the cove. I've only lived here two years."

"Sorry about yer barn fire."

"Thank you for your concern."

"My grandson, Dills here, he's got somethin' to tell ya."

"Grampaw—"

Reid grabbed the boy by the shoulder and shook him. "Don't you 'Grampaw' me. You tell this man, or I'm gonna take the hide off you and give you to the sheriff." He turned back to Anderson. "The boy knows who burnt yer barn."

Reid's grandson stared at the ground.

"Well, tell him."

Silence met the order.

Reid slapped the boy. "Tell him!"

The boy rubbed the back of his head where he had been hit, stalling.

Reid's hand came up fast.

The boy hunched. "All right. All right. Banty Joe Sparks and his brother, Dana."

"Tell him how you know."

The boy twisted away, but the old man grabbed him and spun him back. "Tell him!"

"They offered me fifty dollars to burn yer barn."

Anderson looked at the boy. "Why?"

He said nothing.

Reid slapped the boy in the side of the head. "Tell him."

The boy, hunched again, ventured a peek at Anderson. "They said they heard you was the one who told the sheriff where their still was. They was mad at you 'cause the sheriff busted up their still."

Anderson lifted his shoulders. "I don't even know a Joe Sparks. And I don't know anybody who makes moonshine. I'm a Baptist, as dry as they come."

"Well, they thought—"

"They thought wrong."

Jones came up to the boy. "Did you set the fire, son?"

"No sir. I liked the idee of the money, but I didn't like the idee of jail iffen I was to get caught."

"Do you know where Banty and Dana are?"

"No sir, and that's the God's honest truth." Dills looked up to his grandfather, his eyes pleading.

"That be the truth, Mister Jones, Mister Anderson," Reid said. "Them boys disappeared. Nobody's seem 'em since the fire."

Jones, jingling the keys to his truck in his hand, leaned into Anderson. "Rabun, I've got to call the sheriff on this." He gazed at the boy. "Son, you're gonna have to tell the sheriff what you told us."

"Grampaw—"

"You'll do it, Dills. You shamed us Reids by ever gettin' involved in something like this. And you shamed me by not coming to me right away when we could have stopped this." He gave a jut of his jaw to Jones. "Mister Jones, you have the sheriff come by. Dills will tell him what he knows."

The old man shagged the boy back to the car, ordered him to crank the engine, then the two climbed in and left.

Jones continued to hop his truck keys. "Gawddamn, neighbors burning out neighbors. I thought that was Civil War stuff. Luther, you know where Banty and Dana might be?"

"Grumble, I've not seen 'em for months. But I know my way around the Flats. If they're there, I'll find 'em."

"Well, I got to get home. Rabun, about tomorrow night, I'll round up Dancing Jack Travers. We'll have us some fiddle music and one fine dance in your new barn. I'll even call the squares."

"You're a good friend, Mister Jones."

"Well, I'm just glad you're in our cove. You and your daughter have made an honest man of old Click here, and best, you got him to taking baths regular. He used to come in my store and my customers would run out the other door. Hell, you don't need to know about that." Jones moved away toward where he's left his truck, waving. "See you tomorrow night. Lily and I, we're comin' to dance."

Chapter 5
Chewing tobacco

LUTHER CLICK left the Anderson farm the next morning, walking as was his habit, hoar frost hanging on the trees and a skim of ice covering the stock tank. He took it all in as he moved along toward the road that would take him to the grist mill and Adamson's store that stood across the way from it. The frost and the ice—Luther thrust his hands deep in his pockets and hunched up.

Everyone called it the Adamson's store, although Claude Adamson had died a decade back and Enoch Smith now ran the place. It was small, just a crossroads store, nothing like Grumble Jones' emporium in Townsend. But it stocked the essentials.

A few people came to Adamson's to pick up their mail while most of the cove's farmers got their mail from boxes at the end of their driveways since rural free delivery had come to the cove.

Luther Click still picked up his mail at the store.

"Anything for me, Uncle Enoch?" he asked after he had closed the door behind him, the better to keep the cold out and the heat from Enoch Smith's wood stove in.

"'Bout the only thing is your newspaper from Townsend."

"Have you finished reading it, Uncle Enoch?"

"Yessir, and my wife, too. She read it last night. We thank you, Luther."

"Any news worth our time?"

"Not much."

Luther took the newspaper Smith held out to him and settled on one of the cane-bottomed chairs the storekeeper kept near the stove.

"Sorry about the fire at your father-in-law's place," Smith said as he went back to the stool behind his counter. "Know who may have set it?"

Luther opened the paper to an inside page, to see what the editor was ranting about this week. "Nope. Nobody's talking. You hear anything?"

"Lots of gossip. Nothing you'd want to bet a penny on. Say, friend, last three days, I been watching you and the neighbors through the window, building the new barn. Looks right smart."

Luther glanced up from his reading. "We're gonna have a dance over there, tonight. You and Aunt Til ought to come and clog some after you close the store."

"Thanks for the invite, Luther. We might just do that."

Luther went back to the editor's page. He chuckled to himself as he read.

Enoch looked up from the order pad on which he was making a list. "Something funny there?"

"Editor Montgomery's on a tear. Seems the neighborhood dogs got into the trash pit behind his print shop. Made one awful mess, draggin' garbage all over. Says in his column he's sworn out a warrant for their arrest. Can you picture the constable, old Pete

Clarridge, trying to arrest a pack of dogs?"

Enoch smiled and shook his head.

"Oh Lordy, would you look at this," Luther said, still with his face in the paper. "Romance disaster."

"What's that?"

"Seems a boy from out Wear Cove way got caught in the rain near Nawger Nob. The editor says he sought shelter for the night at the home of H.J. and Grace Wells, that their daughter, Simmy, took a romantic interest in the boy and this scared the boy beyond his wits, she being on the heavy side and none too pretty."

The door creaked open. Luther glanced up as a boy of about eight slipped in. The boy nodded to Luther and went up to Enoch Smith's counter where he took a note and a dollar bill from his jacket pocket.

"Hold that a minute, would you, Luther?" Enoch said. "I got me a fine customer here in young Henry Bridgewater. Everything all right, Henry?"

The boy nodded. He pushed the note and money across the counter.

Luther returned to his reading.

Enoch peered at the note, then went to his shelves and pulled down a plug of Seaton's apple-flavored chewing tobacco and a pair of cotton socks. He set them on the counter, then reached in his trousers' pocket for a handful of coins. Enoch counted out change for the purchase.

Henry Burchfield accepted the coins. He gathered up the goods and left as quietly as he had come in.

Enoch went back to his order pad. "Now what was that you was reading, Luther?"

"The editor says the rain was so bad that Wear

Cove boy had to stay the night, and all he had for sleeping wear was his shirttail. Seems the boy had terrible dreams about what might happen to him. Next morning, when he come down to breakfast, there was the family at the table and one empty chair next to that heavy girl. Says here, as the boy went to sit down, he saw his reflection in the window glass and saw that he hadn't combed his hair, and that was just the hint of things to come. At the table, he dropped his fork, scattered food on the floor, and spilled coffee down the front of his shirt. He was so flustered from all that happened, he decided he'd better just cross his hands in his lap, and that's when he felt the tablecloth across his legs. The editor says the boy thought it was his shirttail and stuffed it into his belt, that when they all got up and left the table, he jerked the dishes on the floor. The editor says the boy managed to fight himself free of the tablecloth and ran for home, leaving the poor girl to look for a less bashful lover who knows his shirttail from a tablecloth."

"Luther, you making that up?"

"A little maybe."

Enoch peered at the piece of paper on his counter for a second time. "Something's not right here."

"What's that?"

"You know that boy that was just in here, Henry Burchfield?"

"No."

"Lives with his grandpap and mamaw up at Chestnut Flats, you know, the Kanatchers?"

"Uncle Ed and Aunt Mapes?"

"That's them. Henry's pap was killed last year, and

the Kanatchers took over raising the boy. Now Uncle Ed grows his own tobacco for chewing—I know he does. He's never bought any. And Henry's here, buying chewing tobacco. And he's buying cotton socks, and I know Uncle Ed wears wool socks year 'round, socks Aunt Mapes knits for him. And so does Henry. Something ain't right."

Luther pushed himself out of the chair. "Well, while you figure it out, I've got to be going. See you, Uncle Enoch."

Luther stuffed his newspaper in his back pocket and slipped out the door.

On the porch, he gazed over at the Seebow Grist Mill, then up the road that led to Chestnut Flats. He saw in the distance the flapping jacket of Henry Burchfield as the boy ran toward home. Luther set out in that direction, shuffling along at his usual leisurely pace, enjoying the sun that now warmed the day.

At the Flats, he turned in the front gate of a shabby house that hadn't seen a paint brush since the day it was built. Luther knocked on a porch post and waited.

A woman, as disheveled as the house, opened the door.

"Banty Joe at home?" he asked.

"My husband?"

"Yes'm."

"No. He went up in the mountains, huntin' fer winter meat."

"When you expect him back?"

"Don't rightly know. After he shoots somethin', I expect." The woman pulled back half a step.

"Oh. Would you tell Banty when he comes home

that Luther Click came by? Tell him I know where he can get a new copper coil cheap."

"How's that?"

"A shiner I know wants to quit the business, and I understand the sheriff busted up Banty's still."

"Luther Click, you say?"

"Yes'm."

She put a hand on the doorjamb. "Well, I'll tell him, Mister Click. 'Course, I don't know when that'll be."

"I understand."

The woman closed the door.

Luther turned away and went further up the road to another house that looked no better. Again he knocked on a porch post. The woman who came to the door held a baby in one arm while a child with no britches clung to her skirt.

"Anna Mae," Luther said, "remember me?"

"Yessir."

"I heard you had little ones." He wiggled his fingers at the child holding tight to the woman's skirt. "Dana at home?"

"No sir."

"Know where I might find him?"

"Gone down to the aluminum reduction plant—to get hisself a job. We're in a hard way."

"So I heard. Understand the sheriff busted up his still."

"Might have."

"Would you tell Dana when he comes home that I know where he can get a new copper coil cheap? Know when that might be?"

"If he gets that job, I expect he might stay down there all winter."

"Could be best. Well, if you don't see him, send him a note, would ya?"

"Can't promise."

"Well, I understand." Luther backed away down the yard. "I won't be bothering you no more. Thank you, Anna Mae."

He waved at the little ones.

Further on, Luther saw the man he really wanted to talk to, digging in his garden—Ed Kanatcher.

"How you doing, Uncle Ed?" he called out.

Kanatcher, bent by age, looked up. He stopped his work and leaned on his grubbing fork. "Oh, I'm surviving. How you, Luther?"

"Tolerable. What are you digging out here for, Uncle Ed?"

"Old Woman sent me out to grub up some turnips. Wants to cook up some for dinner."

"Turnips are good, particularly with a little cured ham."

"Now, Luther, you're makin' an old man hungry. What brings you by?"

"I understand your grandson, Henry, he's living with you now."

"Yessir, 'bout a year."

"Don't suppose he'd like a little work? Pay's fair."

"I expect he might, Luther. What is it?"

"We've been building a barn over at the Anderson place. We got a bunch of picking up and cleaning up to do, and it's about the right-sized job for a boy your grandson's age. He home today?"

"No, he's in school. I could tell him when he gets home. Could you use him tomorrow?"

"I expect we could."

A hand drew back a curtain at an attic window.

Luther glanced up, and the curtain closed. He brought his gaze back to Kanatcher. "How's Aunt Mapes getting' on? Maybe I ought to go in the house while I'm here and say howdy."

"Oh, I wouldn't do that. The Old Woman's got this kind of cold, an' she might give it to you."

"Oh. Well, you greet her for me then, would you? And I'll look to see your grandson tomorrow."

"I expect he'll be there. Boys always need a little money in their jeans' pocket, don't they?"

"They surely do. You take care now."

Kanatcher returned to his digging, and Luther stole another glance at the attic window.

Chapter 6
On the trail of the fire starters

ELROY AND MINNIE Masters arrived first.

"Brought the folding chairs from the Grange hall and the benches from the school," he called down from the buckboard seat of his wagon to Luther and Willy Click, standing in the doorway of the Andersons' barn.

Luther strolled out. "I got to worrying about where we was gonna put everybody. We brought all the chairs out from the house, but that's only a dozen."

"This ought to take care of everybody, and if somebody has to sit on the floor, well, that's just too bad. That Willy I see there?"

The boy beamed.

"You dance, boy?" Masters asked.

"Some."

"Well, you're gonna have a good time, tonight. Right now, help me and your old pap with these chairs and benches. Hand them down for us, would you, Min?"

The men and the boy wrestled chairs and benches into the barn and up the stairs where the Andersons, Janey Leigh and Janey's daughter, Amanda Jane, carried them on and set them up.

"I brought four lanterns, too, Luther. I see you got some hanging up. You want mine?"

"I don't know. Maybe we ought to leave a corner or two dark for the young couples who might want to do some sparking."

"Luther, ever since you got married, you've become a romantic old devil."

"Well, I wouldn't want to deny anybody the joy I've found."

"Luther, Luther." Masters shook his head and reached up to give his wife a hand getting down from the wagon. She reached back for a hamper of food.

"Where you want me to park my rig, Luther?" Masters asked.

"Seems to me if you'd drive around to yon side of the barn, out in the pasture, that's be the best place. I'll try to guide the others to follow you."

"I'll take a lantern with me, the better to see my way back." Masters climbed up to the buckboard seat and handed three lanterns down to Luther. "Send these with Willy upstairs, all right?"

Masters drove his team and wagon away as the next wagon pulled up, Warren and Nancy Ann Sweet on the seat and their children and three neighboring couples in the back. Luther helped them down, then sent Warren and his team and wagon on to follow Masters out into the field.

It went that way for the next half hour. Mid-way through the parade, Grumble Jones drove in in his Kissel, his wife, Lily, in the front seat, and Doc Schroeder and Dancing Jack Travers in the back.

"Seen the sheriff?" Jones asked Luther.

"No."

"Well, damn. He came up on the morning train,

hooked up with Constable Clarridge, and they were going to take Pete's car down to Chestnut Flats. Maybe they're on the trail of Banty and Dana." He thumbed to the backseat of his car. "You see I got Dancing Jack and his fiddle in the back? What say we get this party going?"

"That's what we're all here for." Luther opened the door and helped Travers out. "Good to see you, Jack."

Travers blinked like a barn owl. "Good to see you, too."

Luther nudged the fiddler. "Got your dancing shoes on?"

"Yessir, I even polished 'em. What say we get to it?"

"Just inside and up the stairs."

"All right."

As Travers, with his fiddle under his arm, moved away, Doc Schroeder came around to Luther.

Luther reached out to shake hands. "You don't get to many parties, Doc. Good to see you."

"I've no babies scheduled to be born, and no one in the Tuckaleechee is scheduled to die, so Grumble made me take the night off. Wouldn't even let me bring my black bag, and I keep a bottle in it."

"Oh, I expect you'll find a bottle or two around, maybe even a crockery jug with the good stuff."

Three loud stamps came from the floor above, followed by the scraping of horsehair on cat gut, and that by whoops and hollers.

Schroeder went for the stairs. "I think I'll get me up there and see if your wife will dance with me."

"Janey Leigh'd like that. See, Doc, I don't dance."

"Luther, you will before the end of the night."

"Well, maybe." Luther bobbed his head to Schroeder and turned back to his job of helping new arrivals down from their buckboards and farm wagons.

He was about to go in when a pair of headlights came bouncing up the road toward the farm. A car turned in, Pete Clarridge's Chrysler Runabout. It swayed to a stop in front of Luther. Quill Rose got out from the passenger side.

"Party's started, Quill," Luther said. "You and the constable ought to come on up."

"Might as well. We couldn't find Banty or Dana. Those families on the Flats, they're a clannish bunch and closed mouthed."

"Get to talk to Dills Reid and his grandpap?"

"They gave me the story, but they don't know where the bad boys are. Pete and I went by Banty's and Dana's houses and talked to their wives, but you know Banty and Dana aren't going to be there."

Luther shoved his shoe around in the grass. "I know where they are."

"Really?"

He shrugged. "Just have to know where to look."

"Uh-huh. Where are they?"

"Uncle Ed Kanatcher's attic, hiding."

"I was there. Old Kanatcher didn't let on anything."

"He wouldn't. Banty and Dana are his wife's nephews. They're family, and you're the law."

Rose thumbed his lower lip. "You're sure they're there?"

"Uncle Ed's grandson went in to buy chewing tobacco and cotton socks at Adamson's this morning,

138

and Uncle Ed doesn't chew store-bought tobacco, and his wife knits his socks."

"Who says?"

"Uncle Enoch at the store. So I stopped by, and Uncle Ed lied about his grandson not being home, and he gave me some excuse about why I shouldn't go inside and see Aunt Mapes."

"That's it?"

Luther leaned back, his hands in his pockets. "No. While we were talking out by the garden, somebody opened the attic window curtain. I saw Banty's face before he dropped the curtain back. Don't think he knows I saw him."

"Well, I'll be. I thought I knew how everybody was related to everybody else in the county, but I surely didn't know Aunt Mapes was a Sparks."

"Yeah, old Harv, he was her brother."

"He's been dead, what, a dozen years?"

"About that."

Rose laid a hand on Luther's shoulder. "He'd sure be embarrassed his boys are in trouble."

"Quill, he'd not be embarrassed. He'd be proud."

Quill Rose called to the constable still in the car. "You hear that, Pete? Luther knows where Banty and Dana are. You want to go catch 'em?"

"That's what we come for," Clarridge said.

"Luther, you want to come along?"

"Maybe, if I can bring a rope."

"A rope?"

"Might be useful. We've got a new one in the barn."

"Get it and come along."

THE CONSTABLE killed the headlights and idled on in when he neared Chestnut Flats. "Don't need to announce ourselves," he said to Rose and Luther.

Rose jabbed a finger toward the windshield. "There—there's the Kanatchers' house. Pete, aim off to the edge of the yard."

Clarridge crept the car past the garden. At the end, he turned in.

Rose put his hand on the constable's arm. "Stop here. Kill the engine."

Rose, Clarridge, and Luther got out of the car and eased the doors closed so they wouldn't wake any dogs.

"Your' rope, Luther," Rose whispered.

Luther handed his rope on, and Rose knelt in front of the car. He tied one end of the rope to the car's bumper, then trotted across the way and tied the other end of the rope to the trunk of a tree, tying it at about shoulder level. He glanced up at the moon just as a bank of clouds slid across its face. "Thank you, Lord, we can do without all that light."

On the way back to the car, Rose pushed against the rope. He released it, and it snapped back. "Pete, Luther, there's only three ways to get away from that place—front door, back door, and the side yard. Pete, you take the back door. I'll take the front."

Luther rubbed at his ribs. "What about me?"

"You stay out here. I'm gonna give the boys a chance to do the smart thing. If they don't, Pete and I'll go in and take 'em. If they get past us, you get 'em."

"I'd appreciate it if you didn't let 'em get past you, Quill."

Clarridge reached in through the driver's window. He brought out a shotgun, broke open the barrel and slipped a shell in. "Rock salt. I don't want to kill 'em."

Rose reached in the window on his side of the car and brought out an axe handle. "Pete, just be sure you don't shoot me."

Luther motioned at the axe handle. "That all you gonna use?"

"This is all I need. I can bring a man down with this, and he won't have any holes in him. Let's go, Pete."

Rose, at the front of the house, stepped up on the porch. He banged his axe handle against the side of the house. "Banty Joe? Dana? Shag your butts out here and do it now!"

Bare feet slap against the attic floor, and a voice came. "That you, Quill Rose?"

"It sure isn't the Sunday school teacher! Banty, you coming out, or do the constable and I have to come in and root you out?"

"You think you're up to it?"

"You know I am!"

"I got a gun. I'll shoot ya."

"Better men have tried. Uncle Ed? Aunt Mapes? Henry? You stay in your beds. I know Banty and Dana are in the attic. Don't you get in our way. Pete?"

"Yeah?"

"Let's go get 'em!"

Rose kicked the front door open so hard that, when the door hit the inside wall, the glass shattered.

Clarridge came through the back door, his shotgun

leveled.

Rose saw him. "Easy, Pete, careful where you point that thing."

Clarridge tipped the barrel up toward the ceiling.

"That's better. Now, Pete, the stairs are about three paces away from you. You put a load up there, and we'll give Banty and Dana one more chance to quit."

"I don't like this, Quill."

"I don't like this much either, but it's gotta be done."

Clarridge poked the end of his shotgun around the corner of the stairs and squeezed the trigger. A roar and he whipped the shotgun back and reloaded.

"Banty?" Rose yelled. "Last chance! Next time, we kill you!"

A grunting came from above. A window slid up, and feet slapped down on the roof over the kitchen.

"Oh gawd, he's running!"

Rose raced for the front door and Clarridge the back. Outside, Rose made the turn into the yard as a man leaped the fence at the end of it. "Luther!"

Banty Joe Sparks, pounding hard to put distance between himself and the law, hit the rope hard. His feet ran out from under him, and he slammed down on his back.

Luther Click stepped on his gun hand. "Howdy, Banty. You shouldn'tna burnt my daddy-in-law's barn."

"Luther? Luther, he turned me in."

"He doesn't even know you."

Rose and Clarridge trotted up. Clarridge continued on to his car. He pulled on the headlights, blinding Sparks.

Sparks raised his free hand, blocking the light.

Rose prodded Sparks with his axe handle. "Where's your brother?"

"Inside," Sparks said, his voice strained. "Old Man Anderson shot him. He can't walk."

"Why did you burn his barn?"

"He turned us in."

"You dumb—a county surveyor was down here. He stumbled on your still and told me where to find it. If I'd caught you then, you'd only got six months in the poky. Now it's gonna be ten in Brushfork." Rose turned to Clarridge. "Pete? Get him up. Throw him in the car. Luther and I'll go back for Dana."

Rose and Luther made their way back to the house and around to the front porch where they found Kanatcher and his grandson standing in their long underwear, Kanatcher holding a lantern, his wife huddled behind him, a blanket wrapped around her shoulders.

"Uncle Ed," Rose said, "I'm sorry about breaking your door glass and the constable shooting up your roof. The county will pay for the damage. Banty tells me Dana's still in the attic."

"He is. We picked an awful lot of birdshot out of him. He got hurt awful bad."

"Well, I have to take him to jail."

"I know."

A revolver barked above them.

"Oh gawd—" Rose grabbed Kanatcher's lantern and raced inside. He skidded around the foot of the stairs and pounded his way up. Luther, behind him, stopped at the bottom of the stairs.

A moment later, the light above moved back toward the top of the stairs. The light came into the opening, revealing a haggard Quill Rose. He slumped down on the top step.

"What happened, Quill?"

"He blew his brains out. Now who the hell's gonna take care of his little children?"

ACKNOWLEDGMENTS

This is the fifteenth book I've published as indie author, this one under my Windstar Press imprint.

We indies, loners that we are, nonetheless depend on a lot of people to make our stories and books the best that they can be. Dawn Charles of Book Graphics, a superb cover designer, worked with me on this volume, as she has on several previous books.

Just as a knock-out cover is vital to grabbing potential readers, so are the words on the back cover that say this book is one you really should buy. For those words, I turned to fellow Wisconsin writer Sean Patrick Little. If you're not acquainted with Sean's work, I suggest you read his latest novel, *Lord Bobbins and the Romanian Ruckus*. It's Sean's entry into the world of steampunk fiction, a story you are sure to enjoy.

I always close with a thank you to all librarians around the country. They, like you and your fellow readers who have enjoyed my James Early mysteries, my AJ Garrison crime novels, my John Wads crime novellas, my Wings Over the Mountains novels, and my short story collections, have been real boosters.

A NOTE FROM THE AUTHOR

Looking back over a half-century as a writer, without any doubt it is Wilma Dykeman, the grand dame of Tennessee writers and a master of the short story form, who turned me on to the power of the short story. It was there in her class in graduate school at the University of Tennessee that I wrote the short story that would get me published.

That story centered on Ben and Harold Wright, brothers who lived up in the Smoky Mountains. The time was 1925.

In that story that I titled "The Other Wright Brothers," Ben decides he wants to learn to fly, so he buys a Jenny—that's a World War I biplane—and has it shipped up into the mountains on a railroad flatcar.

One of my fellow students was on the staff of a new literary journal, *Entelechy*. He liked the story so much that he asked me whether I'd let the journal publish it in its premier issue.

Wow, before the end of the semester, before the end of that class, I was a published author!

I've written more than 400 short stories since.

Jerry

WHAT PEOPLE SAY ABOUT MY BOOKS

Early's Fall, a James Early Mystery, book 1 . . . "If James Early were on the screen instead of in a book, no one would leave the room." – Robert W. Walker, author of *Children of Salem*

Early's Winter, a James Early Mystery, book 2 . . . "Jerry Peterson's *Early's Winter* is a fine tale for any season. A little bit Western, a little bit mystery, all add up to a fast-paced, well-written novel that has as much heart as it does darkness. Peterson is a first-rate storyteller. Give *Early's Winter* a try, and I promise you, you'll be begging for the next James Early novel. Spring can't come too soon." – Larry D. Sweazy, Spur-award winning author of *The Badger's Revenge*

The Watch, an AJ Garrison Crime Novel, book 1 . . . "Jerry Peterson has written a terrific mystery, rich in atmosphere of place and time. New lawyer A.J. Garrison is a smart, gutsy heroine." – James Mitchell, author of *Our Lady of the North*

Rage, an AJ Garrison Crime Novel, book 2 . . . "Terrifying. Just—terrifying. Timely and profound and even heartbreaking. Peterson's taut spare style and truly original voice create a high-tension page turner. I really loved this book." − Hank Phillippi Ryan, Agatha, Anthony and Macavity winning author

The Last Good Man, a Wings Over the Mountains novel, Book 1 . . . "Jerry Peterson joins the ranks of the writer's writer—that is, an author other authors can learn from, as in how to open and close a book, but also in how to run the course." − Robert W. Walker, author of *Curse of the RMS Titanic*

Capitol Crime, a Wings Over the Mountains novel, Book 2 . . . "In *Capitol Crime*, Peterson's vivid characters jump right off the page, and his sharp detail and snappy dialog puts the reader right in the middle of Prohibition-era action and one of the wildest schemes ever to take down a bootlegging ring. So buckle up. You're in for a hellava ride!" − J. Michael Major, author of *One Man's Castle*.

Iced, a John Wads Crime Novella, book 1 . . . "Jerry Peterson's new thriller is a thrill-a-minute ride down a slippery slope of suspense and shootouts. Engaging characters, spiffy dialogue, and non-stop action make this one a real winner." − Michael A. Black, author of *Sleeping Dragons*, a Mack Bolan Executioner novel

Rubbed Out, a John Wads Crime Novella, book 2 . . . "Jerry Peterson's latest thriller gives us, once again, an endearing hero, a town full of suspects, and quick action leading to a surprising climax. If you like your thrills to be delivered by strong characters in a setting that matters, this one's for you." – Betsy Draine, co-author with Michael Hinden of *Murder in Lascaux* and *The Body in Bodega Bay*

A James Early Christmas and *The Santa Train*, Christmas short story collections . . . "These stories are charming, heart-warming, and well-written. It's rare today to see stories that unabashedly champion simple generosity and good will, but Jerry Peterson does both successfully, all the while keeping you entertained with his gentle humor. This should definitely go under your tree this season." – Libby Hellmann, author of *Nice Girl Does Noir*, a collection of short stories

A James Early Christmas – *Book 2*, a Christmas short story collection . . . "What brings these Christmas tales to life is the compassion of their protagonist and their vivid sense of time and place. James Early's human warmth tempers the winter landscape of the Kansas plains in the years after World War II. A fine collection." – Michael Hinden, co-author with Betsy Draine of the Nora Barnes and Toby Sandler mysteries

The Cody & Me Chronicles, a Christmas short story collection and more . . . "Jerry Peterson is a fireside tale-spinner, warm and wistful, celebrating what is extraordinary in ordinary people with homespun grace." – John Desjarlais, author of *Specter*

Flint Hills Stories, Stories I Like to Tell – Book 1 . . . "Jerry Peterson's short stories are exactly how short stories should be: quick, but involving; pleasant, but tense; and full of engaging characters and engaging conflicts. I can think of few better ways to spend an afternoon than being submerged in James Early's Kansas." – Sean Patrick Little, author of *The Bride Price*

Fireside Stories, Stories I Like to Tell – Book 3 . . . "Witty and clever, Jerry Peterson spins a tale with a deft pen and an ear for dialogue that you don't find too often. There's an old-fashioned sense of character and craft in Peterson's works that will have you desperate for more." – Sean Patrick Little, author, *The Bride Price*

A Year of Wonder, Stories I Like to Tell – Book 4 . . . "These 24 short gems run the gamut from humorous to mysterious, including a welcome return of Sheriff James Early. You'll wish that a year had more than 12 months in it so that you could have more of these fine stories! A very good year, indeed." – Ted Hertel, Jr., recipient of MWA's Robert L. Fish (Edgar) Award for Best First Short Story by an American author

ABOUT THE AUTHOR

I write crime novels and short stories set in Kansas, Tennessee, and Wisconsin.

Before becoming a writer, I taught speech, English, and theater in Wisconsin high schools, then worked in communications for farm organizations for a decade in Wisconsin, Michigan, Kansas, and Colorado.

I followed that with a decade as a reporter, photographer, and editor for newspapers in Colorado, West Virginia, Virginia, and Tennessee.

Today, I'm back home and writing in Wisconsin, the land of dairy cows, craft beer, and really good books.

COMING SOON

Night Flight, the third book in my Wings Over the
Mountains novels.

Made in the USA
Lexington, KY
11 November 2017